CAPTAIN HARDING AND HIS MEN

CAPTAIN HARDING

AND HIS MEN

Elliott Mackle

Lethe Press

Maple Shade NJ

This is a work of fiction.

This trade paperback edition published by
Lethe Press,
118 Heritage Ave,
Maple Shade, NJ 08052.
lethepressbooks.com / lethepress@aol.com

Cover art by Ben Baldwin
Book Design by Toby Johnson

ISBN-13: 978-1-59021-329-2
ISBN-10: 1-59021-329-7
e-isbn 978-1-59021-417-6

Library of Congress Cataloging-in-Publication Data

Mackle, Elliott J. (Elliot James), 1940-
  Captain Harding and his men / Elliott Mackle.
     p. cm.
  ISBN-13: 978-1-59021-329-2
  ISBN-10: 1-59021-329-7
  1. United States. Air Force--Fiction. 2. Gay men--Fiction. I. Title.
PS3613.A273C33 2012
  813'.6--dc23
                                    2012017115

This book is for
Katharine V. Forrest
Mentor and friend

TABLE OF CONTENTS

Part One

Part Two

PART ONE

CHAPTER 1

MAYDAY

The Lockheed C-130 Hercules taxied into takeoff position at the far end of the north-south runway. The pilot gradually fed power to his four Allison turboprop engines, synchronizing propeller speed and pitch. The low-slung, pug-nose military transport hunched forward like a draft horse straining at the bit, kicking up desert sand and dust, trembling in the late afternoon sun.

Watching from the opposite end of the Wheelus Air Base runway, standing beside our bicycles, Second Lieutenant Ron Connolly and I shrugged and prepared to cover our ears against the coming, screaming whine of the engines. Although the two of us worked out together at least twice a week, I hardly knew the younger man. Biking the marked circuit around Wheelus, Libya, the largest American outpost in Africa, was exactly the kind of low impact, long-distance exercise we both enjoyed. We also jogged a mile or two on the track every third or fourth day. I had a tennis partner as well, but he was away most of the year. On weekends, like any conscientious officer posted overseas, I lifted elbow, downing a lot of tax-free booze at the Officers' Club.

My name's Joe Harding. At the time, October, 1967, I was a captain in the Air Force, serving as executive assistant to the new wing commander, Colonel Mark Earl Swanson. My workout buddy, Lieutenant Connolly, the motor pool officer, was also new on base. Married without children, he'd been drafted a month

11

before graduating from Chicago's Saint Xavier College. Wisely opting for officer's training and clean sheets over humping a grunt's rifle in Southeast Asia, Connolly nonetheless struck me as a slightly dim bulb. Baby-faced, with a dimpled jaw, boyish arms, flat, hairy chest and Midwest twang, he kept his shoes shined and filed his reports on time. His motor-pool troopers had a below-average arrest record and the car and driver assigned to my boss were always ready to roll. In military terms, he easily fit the "Pretty Boy Bean Counter" category. In other words, and aside from conducting official business, I wouldn't have given him much thought.

But after a series of incidents the previous June in which I'd played the hero, the then-acting wing commander, Lieutenant Colonel Bruce Opstein, summarily assigned me the two-room bachelor officer's suite to which I was entitled by rank and position. Connolly took over my single room in the crowded BOQ, sharing a toilet with my buddy, Captain Jeff Masters, the top cop on base. Masters worked out regularly with Colonel Opstein, lifting weights. I thus inherited my buddy's buddy for physical training. We soon fell into a sidekick routine of long, silent jogs and bike rides. The military often works that way, especially overseas.

The Herc's turbocharged engines' familiar, ear-piercing noise increased. Props grabbed air, brakes were released and the plane moved forward, quickly picking up speed, coming toward us. Suddenly, three terrified sheep exploded out of a cactus patch near the runway's midpoint, scampering across the tarmac, turning suddenly and running headlong away from the approaching green monster. They were immediately followed by a barefoot boy waving a stick.

Nose wheels already airborne, halfway down the runway, the airplane braked sharply, shuddered and lurched to the right. Under extreme pressure, the starboard landing gear collapsed. The wingtip struck sand and dug in. The plane pivoted hard. The tip broke off as did the outboard engine. Skidding, trailing a torrent of burning jet fuel and thick black smoke, the plane sliced across the sand in a graceful arc. When it slammed into the base bakery, the flaming fuel ignited the wood-frame, gas-fired structure. By midnight, when I found time to read the rescue and recovery reports stacked on my desk, I learned that two enlisted bakers, three local assistants and the food service officer had died in the fire.

Connolly covered his mouth and then crossed himself. "Mother of God. Jesus, Mary and Joseph. Our father who art in heaven—"

At my previous post, a Strategic Air Command bomber base in California, I'd had three years of disaster-control training. I was essentially hard-wired to initiate any kind of rescue and recovery effort. First man on the scene takes charge and directs the efforts of subordinates; that was the drill. When higher authority arrives, step aside and follow orders.

So I didn't just stand there, much less pray. My training kicked in. "Let's go, Tonto," I shouted. "Mayday."

We hopped on the bikes and took off toward the crash site. Before we'd covered a hundred yards, the forward crew hatch dropped open and the pilot, navigator, enlisted flight engineer and loadmaster exited the burning plane. Moments later, the co-pilot emerged from a hatch above the cockpit and dropped down the side with a life rope.

Behind us, the wail of sirens and hoo-ha klaxons of fire engines, ambulances and air police cars cut the evening air. The air traffic controller in the tower had punched the alarm button moments after the Herc hit the bakery.

Dismounting, we ran toward the crew. As we did so, a beefy man wearing a flight suit bearing neither nameplate, rank insignia or patches stumbled down the hatch steps, almost fell, recovered and began limping toward us. Taller and broader than I am—and I'm a six-three beanpole who stays in shape—he was bleeding heavily from a deep gash across his forehead. Wiping his face and eyes with his hands, he took one look at Connolly, barked, "What in Christ's name—?" pushed Connolly aside with his bloody hands, and rushed past us, his would-be rescuers.

Something inside the plane exploded, blowing out the tempered glass windows and sending plumes of smoke and ash through the open hatches. The wounded man turned back, tried and again failed to wipe the blood out of his eyes, cried, "Ah, fuck! There she goes," and then, waving his arms at all of us, began shouting, "Run, you fuckers, run," as the firecracker pop-pop of exploding ordinance began.

Two fire trucks arrived. Men in yellow suits started hosing flame-retardant foam onto the burning airplane and bakery. One ambulance and then another drew up behind the fire trucks. After signaling the medics that they had wounded to treat, I turned to the flight crew and cut them a salute.

The pilot, a short, trim major with a suntanned face and badly cut ear, ignored me. Instead, he grabbed the taller man and stopped him by sheer force. "What about your passenger? He still in there?"

"Look like his neck was broke, Clint. Yeah. Fucker hadn't fastened his fucking belt. Hit the bulkhead. Hard."

"You just left him?"

"He was dead, Clint. What the fuck? You hear what I'm saying?"

"The boss, he's not—"

"Shut your face, Clint. Get your shit together."

"It's my airplane and he, you, you—"

Medics in whites and air police in camo surrounded the two injured men, deftly separated them and led them toward separate ambulances. Inside the burning airplane the explosions continued. Suddenly, the wind shifted, blowing thick, oily smoke in our faces. The firemen and their hoses briefly retreated. So did we.

Jeff Masters and Lieutenant Colonel Opstein, who had resumed his primary duty as deputy commander for operations, arrived in a Jeep, direct from the gym. Clad in blue workout shorts and sweat-soaked USAF T-shirts, their arms, necks and shoulders pumped up like supermen, they might have been father-and-son bodybuilders. Both were straight, married and moderately religious. Ops wore glasses, shaved his scalp and resembled an athletically inclined rabbi or math teacher. Jeff, with buzz-cut black hair and leather wristbands, looked like what he was: an Arkansas cop whose favorite reading material was *Playboy*. Jeff was one of my closest friends and, in very different ways, we both worshipped Ops. Ops, in turn, knew our secret vices and ignored them. At its best, that's the way the Air Force worked.

Ops took over rescue and fire-control efforts. Jeff directed his troops to begin securing the area. Medics stowed the injured men in separate ambulances and drove away.

Lieutenant Connolly suddenly appeared at my side. Under a light coating of oil and smoky dust, his face had turned pale gray.

"There were people in that building, Joe. The fire chief told me. They couldn't get to them."

"You OK, Ron?"

He nodded once, looking past my ear, seemingly in some kind of shock. I figured he'd never come so close to violent death before. "Yes, sir."

"You know that guy?" I said. "One with the cut forehead?"

Connolly glanced down, recovered. "No. Don't think so. He must of took me for somebody else." He swung his arms, shook his head and tried to brush the blood off his golf shirt. "Never seen him before. No. No, sir."

Connolly wasn't a very good liar. His boyishness betrayed him. Baby face aside, he suddenly struck me as essentially adolescent, badly shaken by violent death but also worried, guilty and working hard to keep his trap shut.

Behind me, shouts and cheers. Turning, I saw a dozen firemen pumping victorious fists in the air. The fires were out. Other troopers could move in and begin investigating the causes and effects of the disaster.

The wing commander, Colonel Swanson, finally arrived in his staff car. I put Connolly out of my mind. Swanson, a former B-36 pilot, was six-one, a solid one-eighty-five pounds, with close-cropped silver hair, narrow, prominent jaw and grey-blue eyes that could spot a bent antenna or pair of unshined oxfords a thousand yards away. Although he hadn't been scheduled to fly that day, he was dressed in a starched-and-pressed flight suit, blue garrison cap and lace-up boondockers.

His voice low and measured, he asked to be briefed. The co-pilot, still standing but clearly exhausted, described the plane's initial roll, rotation, maximum speed, the sheep and shepherd suddenly appearing out of nowhere, the abort and landing gear failure—an oft-noted fault of the A-model C-130, he explained—the pivot and collision with the now-destroyed bakery and the crew's successful exit from the burning plane. Surprisingly, he didn't mention the missing passenger. Connolly didn't speak up, either, so I decided save it for later. After all, I didn't actually know that anyone else, alive or dead, had been aboard; I'd only heard it mentioned.

Connolly and I confirmed what the co-pilot had said. Ops and Jeff outlined their recovery and security plans. The fire chief heartily praised his own troops' skillful use of obsolete equipment.

Speaking in somber, measured tones, the old man praised us all for our efforts and issued new orders. Secure the crash site, he said. Collect remains and convey them to the base hospital. But initiate no investigation until clear instructions are received from higher authority.

"And until you hear different," he added, "do not discuss this incident with anyone—not your wives, not your buddies, talk to no one from off base."

What was going on? Ordering that the incident be put under wraps was surprise number two. What dangerous cargo had the transport been hauling, I wondered, and where was it headed? Sure, there was the war in Vietnam, not to mention assorted ongoing conflicts in the Middle East. But I'd previously helped debrief a number of air crew members who'd narrowly escaped buying the farm. What I'd heard and seen just now didn't add up. Instinctively, I didn't trust this crash. And it worried me.

Wheelus, seven miles east of Tripoli and situated on the narrow strip of land that separates the Sahara and the Mediterranean Sea, was built as Mellaha Air Base by the Italians in the nineteen-twenties. Used by the Luftwaffe during World War Two, it was captured by the British in January, 1943, and immediately turned over to the United States Army Air Forces. Since then, Wheelus had served a variety of purposes: forward base for the invasion of Europe; refueling stop for transports, operational base for bombers, fighters, tankers and air-rescue helicopters; weapons training center and jump-off point for clandestine operations in Africa and the Middle East.

By the time I arrived in 1966, the principal mission was training. Europe-based American and NATO fighter squadrons flew down TDY—that's military-speak for temporary duty—set up shop in a sunny locale famed for good flying weather, and practiced air-to-air combat, air-to-ground gunnery and what's delicately termed "ordinance delivery" over a bombing range in the empty desert eighty miles southeast of Wheelus. They brought with them not only pilots and mechanics but administrators, weapons specialists and, occasionally, wives and girlfriends. We supplied housing, hangars, a hospital and chapel, mess halls, clubs and as much jet fuel as the squadron commanders demanded. For all intents and purposes, Wheelus was a very large summer camp with a filling station attached.

And I was executive assistant to the man in charge of the whole darned thing.

After a brief stop at the BOQ to shower and put on a uniform, I hauled ass to headquarters. Colonel Swanson wasn't there but the air police guards on the main entrance were. I don't like surprises; no career officer does. When questionable situations do arise, anyone plotting an orderly rise from junior officer to brigadier general must gather vital information as quickly and discreetly as possible. Like any wise administrator, I collected and saved bits of intelligence which might prove useful later. I called them my get-out-of-jail-free cards.

I therefore asked one of the APs to find my chief clerk, Airman First Class Ellwood "Buster" Wilson, and send him to me ASAP.

Wilson strolled in ten minutes later, set a Dixie cup and a disposable wooden spoon on my desk and saluted. He was dressed for the un-air-conditioned chow hall: baggy Bermuda shorts, sandals and a wide-striped T-shirt.

"Figured you'd be one hungry man after putting them fires out, Boss. Ice cream was the easiest lift."

"We're not supposed to talk about that. Colonel's orders."

"Everybody knows, Boss. Unless maybe they're in the lock-up ward at the hospital. Kind of hard to ignore a crashed airplane. My barracks still smells like smoke." He pointed at the ice cream. "All they had was banana."

"All they ever have is banana."

"Yes, Boss. The sadeeks, they like the banana. They hate chocolate, vanilla and pistachio. The sadeeks run the fake-milk plant."

We called the locals sadeeks, the Arab word for *friends*. Most Libyans weren't our friends at all. We inherited the hatred earned by their former Italian and Turkish overlords. I tried to avoid thinking about what terms they applied to us.

"Thanks, but we've got work to do. Sorry to call you in on short notice."

Wilson reached inside his shirt sleeve and scratched his armpit. His sideburns needed a trim and he was one of those dark, husky men who need to shave twice a day to be presentable. Not yet twenty-three, he was already developing a paunch.

"I had a date with Ursula Andress, Boss. They were flying her in special. Don't let your ice cream get cold. What's up?"

Wilson looked like a slob who didn't finish high school. In fact, he was a filing and paperwork whiz who could type one hundred and twenty words a minute and was cleared higher than top secret.

"We're not supposed to talk about this. You understand?"

"Yes, Boss."

"I want you to taxi over to flight ops and pick up some papers for me."

"Piece of cake. Glad to do it. What papers?"

"The thing we're not supposed to talk about. I need to see the flight plan and manifests—cargo, crew and passenger lists, whatever you can put your hands on. There should be carbons. Lift one each."

"They gonna let me?"

"They know who you work for. Any questions, you tell them to call me. I'll be here."

Wilson returned with a handful of carbon flimsies in under an hour. By then, Colonel Swanson was huddled with Colonel Opstein and two flight controllers in his private office. I'd been told to get the USAFE duty officer in Germany on the secure phone but couldn't get through. That took priority. I had to keep trying.

"I took 'em ice creams," Wilson said. "They was glad to get 'em. Even banana."

Wilson was not only smart, he was devious. I like that in a man. I wondered how soon I'd be able to get him promoted to staff sergeant.

I told Wilson to copy the documents in the mailroom down the hall, stash the copies in my desk's top drawer, secure the originals in my safe and take off.

After Colonel Swanson and the others left the office, I was able to read through the copies. According to the manifest, the dead passenger turned out to be someone I'd met at the American embassy. Listed as Mr. Pierre L. Ferrette, Pete Ferrette was officially the US trade representative to Libya. My security clearance was such that I knew his real role: CIA station chief. Although I didn't know him well, he'd made a definite impression: slim, mid-forties with a dark crew cut and white sidewalls, invariably clad in blacks and grays, a clever man and very single. I spotted him as a closeted gay the first time I met him. We had little reason to interact beyond small talk at embassy receptions and I'd kept it that way.

The tennis partner I mentioned was Ambassador Elizabeth Boardman's seventeen-year-old son, a boarding-school boy nicknamed Cotton. We'd started playing and swimming laps together the previous year and quickly become friends. Once the boy developed a serious crush on me, things got complicated. I liked the boy just a little too much. I'd had to work hard to keep my hands to myself without hurting his feelings.

Ferrette, I knew, had the ambassador's ear. If he'd recognized me as a camo-homo, and I'd done the slightest thing to cross him—turn down a pass, say, which luckily had not been made—he might have shared his suspicions with the ambassador, his CIA handlers or anyone else with something to trade.

Fuck, I thought. *There's no telling what he may have thought or guessed or said. He might have left a diary or notes in his quarters, talked to one of the men I'd actually had sex with, or just watched me and the boy enjoying each other's company. He might have imagined I was some kind of pedophile predator. After all, he was a spy by trade.*

If the ambassador suspected I'd fooled around with her precious son—and I definitely hadn't—my career would be over and I might never see Cotton again. Or at least not until after I got out of the military prison at Fort Leavenworth.

The flight plan and cargo manifest, contained yet another surprise. The plane was en route from Dover AFB, Delaware to Korat AFB, Thailand. The cargo was listed as medical supplies and avionics replacement parts, an obvious fiction. Having spent three years on a bomber base, I was well aware that bandages, drugs, copper wires and radio tubes were unlikely to explode with the force that destroyed the C-130.

Finally, paging through the copies for the third time, I realized that there was no crew list. The pilot's name, Gordon S. Stein, was printed and scrawled on the flight plan. The name I'd heard him called, Clint, didn't fit any of that.

Early the next morning, an Air Force C-135—the military version of the Boeing 707—arrived from the States. The first we knew of its arrival was when the pilot radioed the Wheelus tower for permission to land. Colonels Swanson and Opstein were rousted out and met the plane on a taxiway near the burned-out C-130. They were handed Department of the Air Force orders directing them to assist and support the newly arrived crash-investigation team's efforts to collect and photograph evidence and to prepare the dead passenger's body for shipment home.

Verbal orders by the team chief followed: little or no assistance or support would be required. Bottom line: Back off, gentlemen, this is way above your pay grade.

I was standing just behind the old man and Colonel Ops. It was all I needed to hear. Within thirty minutes, Airman Wilson was on his way back to flight ops with the carbon flimsies. Thirty minutes later, he returned to the office, a baffled look on his face. He reported that the original documents had disappeared and that yesterday's doomed flight was now listed as a Dover-Wheelus-Dover round trip commanded by one Major G. S. McClintock. No cargo, crew or passenger lists were on file at all. He'd quietly made copies of the new documents on the spot.

"So what do we do with these flimsies, Boss? And the black-and-whites I just made? Something funny's going on, looks like to me."

I thought fast. "Call the locksmith. Get him over here now. Tell him to change the combination on my safe. This stuff is all top secret, you understand? Don't mention it to anybody. Even the colonel."

"Loose lips sink ships, Boss. Gotcha. It's done."

"When you give me the combination, I'll stash the papers. And you can plan to take Monday off."

"YES, Boss."

The crash team worked fast. When the C-135 took off a few minutes past sunset, a flag-draped casket was aboard. So were the C-130's flight crew, the patched-up mystery man in the unmarked flight suit and twelve large cartons containing the charred residue of everything that could be removed from the interior of the burned-out Herc.

I was under no illusion that everything I heard, read or saw in the military was what it seemed. There might be some reasonable explanation for the substituted documents. In wartime, anything goes.

I had no proof that Pete Ferrette was in that casket or even dead. Still, I was keenly aware that I knew things that other people didn't know I knew, things they didn't want me to know and might hurt me for knowing—hurt me or worse.

So I did the only reasonable thing. I phoned Jeff Masters and told him the drinks were on me. The two of us hit the club bar at five minutes past quitting time. We carefully didn't talk about the past twenty-four hours. We didn't need to. Without actually discussing the accident in any detail, we swiftly agreed that we'd just witnessed some very major cover-up.

A couple of weeks later, a memo arrived from the personnel office stating that my required annual marksmanship qualification was overdue. Routed through the air police station, it carried a note from Jeff saying that he'd personally reserved the shooting range for oh-seven-hundred hours the following Tuesday and would supply weapons and ammo.

On the appointed day and time, Jeff and I turned out to be the only scheduled shooters. Tech Sergeant Ward, Jeff's first sergeant and a crack shot with a rifle, served as range master. Like Jeff, Sergeant Ward looked like what he was: a graduate of South Central Los Angeles, the son of a single mother determined to keep him off drugs and out of trouble until he was old enough to kiss Watts goodbye. Physically, he resembled a Masai warrior clad not in robes but in green utilities, spit-shined brogans and aviator shades. His skin was dark chocolate, his hair a dull Titanium black, his arms and legs longer than mine. He had a high waist, tin can butt and narrow shoulders that accented an oval head smaller than it might have been. He didn't smile a lot. The ribbons on his chest proved that he knew how to cause trouble for the enemy. I was glad he was on our side.

Colt .45-caliber, semi-automatic pistols were the regulation sidearm for non-flying officers and cops. Jeff and I shot half a dozen rounds to test the Colts' kick and to get our hand-eye coordination in trim. Then we shot for real. I forget the precise number of torso shots and heart-stoppers required. Qualification scores changed over the years. Anyhow, when we were done I was confident I'd shot well enough.

As Ward filled out my score sheets he looked up a couple of times and shook his head approvingly.

"Captain Harding," he finally said, "you just earned yourself a expert marksman's ribbon. Congratulations."

I'd shot better than well enough, and not for the first time. "Actually, Sergeant, I already own it," I answered. "Qualified four, five years ago. On my first try after ROTC."

Jeff looked surprised. His ribbon rack didn't include this one. Most Air Force people didn't even know what the blue and green ribbon signified, or care. Ward and I knew and did care. We both wore it.

"Yes, sir. Pardon me for not recognizing that fact. I guess you could hold your own against a bunch of gooks, sir."

"I'd trade it for ya'lls' Vietnam service medals any day. Stuck in this desert backwater flying a desk in headquarters."

Jeff began wiping down his Colt with a cloth. "Backwater where you already earned the Air Force Commendation medal and a Purple Heart."

Jeff was referring to the series of incidents earlier that year involving himself, Colonel Opstein and me. Together we'd stopped a deranged pilot from attacking an Arab warship during the run-up to the Six-Day War, thereby helping keep the United States out of the conflict. Ops recommended the medal and pushed it through. Ambassador Boardman insisted on the Purple Heart, awarded for injury in battle. Her son and I were badly burned when a Molotov bomb-throwing mob attacked the embassy that same week. Assisted by Jeff and Sergeant Ward, we essentially saved each other. I thereby earned not only another medal but a regular place on the ambassador's guest list. Like I said before, I wanted to stay on her good side.

"Ya'll came back from Nam with your own medals and stars and commendations and what? Scalps? Mummified fingers? French jewelry for your wives?"

Jeff scowled. "I didn't bring back nothing but a bad case of crotch rot. Day after I got to Arkansas, I burned all of it in the backyard—stinking uniforms, mildewed boots, muddy cunt cap, even the magazines I'd read on the plane. Bought new everything at the base exchange. The wife bitched about a waste of good money. I wanted to forget what I'd seen, where I'd been. You know that, Joe."

I did know. Jeff occasionally woke up punching the walls of his room. In any BOQ or barracks, post-Nam nightmares weren't all that uncommon. No term existed for it then—shell shock came closest—but a whole generation of airmen, soldiers, nurses and medics went home changed, and many not for the better. Some lived their lives as walking wounded. Others, like Jeff, coped and soldiered on and sometimes cried out in the night. I'd talked him through more than a few bad spells and terrifying flashbacks.

And now I'd bested him before his top NCO. Jeff's scores bought him another year of grace but no distinction. I chose my words carefully.

"I guess any one of us could take out a few Cong in a firefight. Am I right, Jeff? Sarge?"

Ward spoke up. "Sir, if you don't mind my asking, how'd you learn to shoot so good?"

I'd wondered if he'd ask. "My uncle Carl. He's the man that raised me. He has a farm outside Ocala. He started me out on a .22-caliber rifle. When you've got domestic animals and wildlife around, you have to be able to handle a firearm."

"Yes, sir. That's what I been told."

"Then I shot some in college, ROTC rifle team."

"Cool."

"The only pistol I ever handled before college was a Roy Rogers cap pistol. But the theory's the same. Sight, draw a breath, hold it, squeeeeze the trigger."

"Yes, sir!"

After the qualification forms were completed, signed and witnessed, Jeff introduced the real reason for the meeting. He invited Ward to repeat a story he'd told him a few days earlier. This is what he said.

A month ago, Ward explained, a C-130 en route from Dover, Delaware, to Korat Air Base, Thailand, was damaged during an otherwise routine refueling stop. A fuel truck driven by a local had collided with a propeller, damaging the prop and shaft badly enough to require replacement. The pilot, aware of the nature of the cargo he was hauling, informed base operations that the plane needed to be unloaded before it could be tugged into a hangar and serviced. A squad of APs, led by Ward, was called to secure the area. During the unloading process, another local, this one operating a forklift, managed to drop a wooden crate from a height of six or seven feet. When the crate hit the tarmac it smashed open. Half a dozen British 81 millimeter mortars spilled out. A disaster control team was summoned to take charge. The mortars were later repacked and, once the C-130 was repaired, sent on their way.

Aside from newly minted British weapons being transported from the US to Southeast Asia on an American Air Force plane, there was nothing particularly unusual about the series of events. Still, I wondered why I was unaware of the accident. Some kind of paperwork ought to have crossed my desk.

And Korat, Thailand, rang all sorts of bells, ones Jeff didn't yet know about.

Last week, Jeff continued, Sergeant Ward pulled replacement guard duty at Wheelus's main gate. Ward routinely filled in vacant slots, demonstrating his gung-ho willingness to share his troops' duties and dangers.

Ward picked up the tale. "During the shift, sir, we stopped this covered deuce-and-a-half-ton truck from the motor pool for routine inspection. Now this particular truck was preparing to exit the base, sir, and it was being driven by the motor pool officer in charge, Lieutenant Connolly."

I couldn't help breaking in. "Which was definitely not routine?"

"No, sir. But what really set us back a step, he had a Air Force NCO in a flight suit riding shotgun. Didn't look right. So I told my men to open up the cargo area and check it out."

This smelled funnier and funnier. "What did you find, Sergeant? Canned hams? Whisky? Banana ice cream?"

Ward didn't crack a smile. "Four cases of Armour corned beef hash, number ten cans, six to the box; eight cases of Pet canned milk, also number tens, and two wooden packing crates that didn't differ in any respect from that busted up crate containing the mortars from the C-130. Serial numbers was probably different is all."

"You asked him about his cargo?"

"Yes, sir. He waved a set of papers at me, said he was under orders not to discuss the matter. Told me he was directed by higher authority. Told me I wasn't cleared to see the paperwork."

"And so you let him go?"

"No choice in the matter, sir. When the truck returned two hours later, the NCO was driving and Lieutenant Connolly was riding."

"And the cargo bed was empty?"

"You got that right, Captain. I took the matter directly to Captain Masters. Soon as the shift was done."

Jeff looked dead serious. "So it looks to me like we either got a severe breach of security on our hands or grand theft of government property, maybe both. Wanted to run the whole nine yards past you before initiating any kind of official investigation, hauling Connolly in for questioning, going to my boss, Colonel Ops, or the fucking OSI"—meaning the Office of Special Investigations, the Air Force secret police.

After telling them to sit tight for twenty-four hours, I headed for the office. As usual, Airman Wilson's uniform looked like an un-ironed laundry bag. He still needed a haircut. But his desk was clear and his eyes looked like he'd slept all night so I quickly issued instructions: Comb through the previous ten days' orders and directives and all the most recent classified bulletins, messages and instructions for any mention of case lots of corned beef hash, evaporated milk or weapons and ordinance. Finishing well before quitting time, he found no authorization for Connolly's *sub rosa* delivery.

Jeff and I confronted Connolly at the motor pool the next morning. His initial answers ranged from evasive to "I don't recall."

Jeff got specific. "Armour corned beef hash, Lieutenant. Canned milk. Wooden crates containing unidentified objects, most likely weapons or ordinance. You want me to get sworn statements from my troopers? Witnesses."

Connolly's shoulders dropped but he didn't say anything.

"Who was the NCO riding shotgun?"

"Don't know his name, sir."

The cords in Jeff's muscular neck tightened visibly as he dropped his voice from properly official to menacing. "Bullshit, Ron. We could be talking grand theft, government property here. Feels to me like it's time to read you your rights."

Connolly wilted and fessed up, sort of. "Not allowed to discuss the matter, sir. Ordered not to, sir. Concerns the security of the United States of America. Sir."

"Ordered by who?"

"Not allowed to say, sir."

"Fine. Then we'll go up the line to your supervisor, Colonel Ops."

Connolly looked at me imploringly, as if hoping I might rescue him. He was dumber than I'd thought. "Your call, Ron. You talk or we walk—to base ops and then maybe around the corner to the OSI."

Connolly lit a Camel—a blunder, a move completely out of order for a second lieutenant being grilled by superior officers. Compounding the error, he offered us the pack. We declined.

"All I can say, gentlemen, is, well, this was the third time I'd been handed a set of classified, eyes-only, USAF orders by a loadmaster or co-pilot transiting Wheelus. In each case I was contacted by a member of a flight crew on the ground, directed to requisition a truck and collect certain items. In each case I was verbally instructed to drive into town and wait in some public place—the Uaddan Hotel this last trip—while the other man delivered the cargo someplace else."

Jeff's hands were clasped together in front of his chest, pushing, pulling and pumping up his arms in frustration. "You gave unidentified individuals the use and possession of your trucks? Three different fucking times?"

Connolly ducked his head, meaning yes.

"Did you retain copies of the orders?"

"No, sir. I wasn't allowed to do that."

"Was the air crew always the same?"

"Don't know, sir. Only saw one man per shipment, all different."

"And you didn't consult your superior officer, Colonel Opstein, when this thing got to be a habit?"

"No, the orders was clear on that."

"And you didn't report the incidents to anyone?"

"Like I said, sir, I was ordered not to." Connolly sucked deeply on the Camel, stubbed out the butt and blew the smoke away from us. "Sir," he added as if in mitigation, "the Connolly clan motto is 'Faithful to Pledges.' My life as an officer and gentleman is bound by that."

You've seen too many bad movies, I thought but didn't say. "When you raised your right hand," I said instead, "you pledged to be faithful to the Constitution, the Commander in Chief and your own immediate superiors, not a string of nameless yo-yos."

"Roommate," Jeff added quietly, almost sadly. "You been set up."

"Captain Masters may not agree," I said pointedly, "but it sure looks to me like you could be charged with transporting contraband British weapons in violation of various treaties and UN mandates. Not to mention removing valuable government property from the base without your commander's knowledge or consent."

"What the surprise is to me," Jeff said, mild again, "is that that A-model Herc that ate the bakery hasn't come around to bite your ass. Not yet, anyhow."

"What—what do you mean?"

"Whoever organized this canned milk and mortars operation, you were the stooge set to take the fall if it blew up worse than it did. You get my meaning now, son?"

What I got was that the whole affair was a hornets' nest just waiting to be poked with a sharp stick. Jeff and I were in it up to our armpits. We had to protect ourselves—and Ops—from collateral damage if the hornets decided to sting. The three of us owed each other plenty—loyalty, honesty, confidentiality and, in Jeff's and my cases, obedience and information. This could turn into a circle-the-wagons situation. I was anxious as hell and I wanted to work through it fast.

Shifting my tone from bad cop to bike buddy, I asked Connolly if he remembered or could reveal any other details—type of aircraft, tail numbers, dates, cargo transported.

"Funny, yeah. They were all C-130 Hercs, all Air Force. But one tail number stuck in my head. It ended with 007, like in James Bond. You know?"

Of course I knew. Every military man knew. The James Bond movies drew cheering, macho crowds at posts, camps, bases and on allied warships around the world.

Connolly ducked his sorry head again. "Nothing else comes to mind, though."

Again it was obvious that he was lying.

I put Airman Wilson back on the trail, asked him to quietly check flight operations for patterns and repeats, including transports with tail numbers ending in 007, flight plans, crew lists and transits. Not surprisingly, there was a short mountain of paperwork on the wrecked and salvaged Hercules. So I wondered out loud how many other planes from the crashed plane's unit at Dover transited Wheelus or filed flight plans to Korat, Bangkok or the like.

"Compare from the original flimsies in the safe," I cautioned him. "Not the fakes."

"Piece of cake, Boss. Glad to do it."

It took Wilson a couple of days. The crashed Herc had overnighted and refueled at Wheelus on at least one previous trip to Korat, according to a flight plan on file. A loadmaster named Pouncy landed at Wheelus on at least two such missions.

The day after Wilson briefed me, Jeff and I quietly confronted Connolly on the running track.

Jeff skipped the preliminaries. "Are you acquainted with an NCO named Pouncy? Been through here a time or two?"

Connolly shrugged and shook his head and smiled that innocent Irish smile that so often disguises lying Irish blarney.

"No, Captain. Not as far as I know. No."

I turned bad cop again. "You didn't recognize any of the survivors on that crashed Herc?"

The smile died. "No, no. Didn't you ask me that before?"

"The man with the cut-up face. He spoke to you, recognized you, it looked like."

Connolly refused to say more, contending that he'd said too much already, that he'd been ordered to say nothing at all, and implying that Jeff's and my repeated questions about classified operations were way out of line.

His lies were obvious and impossible to ignore. I went to Colonel Opstein the next day. Loyal to his men, and not yet personally committed to serving the new wing commander, he ran a watered-down version of events by Colonel Swanson, classing it, he told me later, as barracks rumor and undigested scuttlebutt.

Swanson, reliably informed that the sharp-eyed Opstein kept tabs on everything, replied that it had all been an off-the-books operation, highly classified deliveries to NATO vessels in Tripoli harbor, not a Wheelus matter at all, and to forget about it.

"We merely facilitated delivery," Opstein quoted him as saying. "And it's already been shut down."

When Ops took me aside at the club that night he added, "It was headed up by people a lot higher the food chain than wing or even USAFE. And now they've turned the lights out."

That's good news, I answered. And I hoped it was true. But I doubted it.

Given that a delivery had occurred only a few days earlier, Jeff doubted it, too. We again took Connolly aside, this time in their shared BOQ over a bottle of Spanish brandy.

Without repeating all that Ops had told me, I suggested that Connolly consult Jeff or even me if another such set of orders was produced.

Connolly countered. He'd thought it over, he said. If it happened again, he'd refuse to cooperate without orders from his own boss, Colonel Opstein.

"I'm nobody's fall guy, OK? I'm from Chicago, see? I got my own ass to cover and a wife to support. Nobody's gonna catch my dick in the wringer."

Jeff said that sounded like a plan. I refilled everybody's glass and we toasted Connolly's resolve. At that point I wouldn't have traded places with the hapless lieutenant for a general's silver stars. I also figured that Jeff and I were well out of it.

CHAPTER 2

WHAT CHILD IS THIS

"Y ou hurt me, Joe," Cotton Boardman whispered. "It still aches. God, I didn't think—"

"You said you'd done things."

"Not like that. Except with one guy, Qamar, the tennis player in Delhi, but he was about half your size. And he hurt me a lot, too, down there. Getting caught with Qamar's what got me sent to boarding school. He—"

"Kiddo, I didn't mean to hurt you. Do you want to go back to the room? See if you're bleeding or something?"

"No. I want to eat my omelet and *frites*—if they'll ever bring it—and have a second glass of wine. And then go back to the room and find out if what I want to do to you will work out any better. I promise, I won't hurt *you*."

I sipped my coffee. If I'd started in on wine, I'd have gotten blind drunk. My embarrassment and frustration would drive me to it. "Cotton, you can't ever hurt me. Learning about each other is going to take time." I swabbed butter onto a crust of French bread and bit into it. "Maybe we ought to go to a clinic."

"Yeah, sure. Doctor, this is my uncle, the Air Force captain. I just happen to have sat on the wrong end of a tennis racquet this morning. No, really, could it be too many prunes, or—"

"You want to keep your voice down?"

"Why? You didn't. When you were—when I was begging you to stop and you wouldn't even give me a breather. They could have heard you in the next hotel."

In in my short life I'd made a lot of stupid mistakes, mostly sex mistakes, thinking with my balls instead of my brain. This was the worst fuck-up yet. I wasn't sure I even deserved a second chance to make it right with Cotton.

The ambassador's son was seventeen; I was ten years older. In late November he'd written me from his boarding school at Gstaad to say that his mother was returning to Washington for talks over Christmas, that he saw no point in flying to the States where he had no friends, and that I ought to join him in Switzerland. I hadn't consciously planned to take him to bed. I loved the boy and wanted to wait. We were friends, I'd told him, and told myself. Trust the friendship, I'd said. We'll be together when we can be, I'd promised. When you're old enough. When you're legal—legal, that is, within the convoluted moral universe I'd constructed for myself out of classics and philosophy books, the so-called honor code mouthed by the Southern gentry class from which I sprung, and years of hands-on schooling by an older mentor at Vanderbilt. The mentor, now a married preacher in Chattanooga, had plenty to say about the ethics of erotic love and the glories of manly friendship. But on the day of his wedding he left me drunk, alone and far from home, my car in a ditch. Somehow, I felt as if I'd done the same thing to Cotton.

I'd arrived in Gstaad late the night before and left a message at his fancy school, Le Rosey. When Cotton knocked on my hotel room door that morning, I hadn't shaved, showered or dressed. It didn't matter. We hugged and slapped each other's backs. And laughed and hugged again. The slaps became caresses, the hug an embrace, the welcoming words an unstoppable flood of sighs and kisses. *He's almost eighteen,* I told myself as I unbuckled his belt. *Next time I see him, he will be. He said he's done this before. It's OK. No one will know.*

"You wouldn't stop." Cotton drained his glass of pale-gold Fendant and looked around, hoping to catch the waiter's eye. "You were practically shouting. 'Oh God, oh sweet, oh Cotton, my little boy, we're one man, we are, oh God.'" The waiter crossed the room, delivered a plate of bread to another table, glared at what must have looked and sounded like a pair of American perverts and fled back to the kitchen.

Although I loved Cotton more than my own life, at that moment I wanted to strangle him and then shoot myself. Above us, through a window, blinding white snow covered the rocky Alps like swirled frosting on a rough-hewn cake. Bing Crosby's "White Christmas" smarmed from unseen speakers. I hated the sanctimonious crooner. I hated those frigid European mountains even more.

Cotton was right. I should have listened when, almost crying, he whispered, "I love you, but you're hurting me. Fuck. Stop. Ow, Jesus. Take it out. Please."

I should have gone easy. The boy didn't know how to relax and I didn't know to teach him. Hell, in those days, many gay men, myself included, knew next to nothing about warming up another man, stretching him with fingers and tongue, readying him for what was considered real lovemaking. No, it was usually just grease-and-go, if that. Or spit.

I'd at least applied Vaseline. But I'd also lost control and satisfied nobody. Did he really need medical attention? He was right, how would we explain such a thing to a doctor in a Swiss emergency room?

For a long moment I couldn't speak. My emotions were in overdrive: shame, disappointment, fear that I'd badly injured him, the real danger of exposure combined with the searing possibility of losing this very special young man forever.

"With rue my heart is laden, Crane."

"*The droughte of march hath perced me to the roote*, Hawk. Get it, Chaucer, *Canterbury Tales,* line two, get it?"

We had butch-cute nicknames for each other. "Crane" referred to Cotton's flapping arms and long-legged, galumphing gait on the tennis court, "Hawk" to my status as bloodthirsty war monger. In private we often used literary and classical allusions, a happy meeting of minds which bound us together.

"I get it, Geoffrey. *And bathed every veyne in swich licour, Of which vertu engendred is the flour.* Lines three and four."

"OK, bravo. So 'with rue'—who?"

"A.E. Houseman. You don't know him? A Brit. My mother's favorite poet. He was one of us. Studied classics, became a Latin scholar."

"Oh, I thought you meant—"

"That, too. His poems are mostly coded, rose-lipt lasses for lightfoot lads. But the lad he loved all his life was a straight jock who wouldn't have him."

Cotton rolled his eyes. "I'm sure learning a lot from you today."

"Crane, I'm sorry. How many times do I—?"

"Just forget it. I'm tough. You know? It doesn't ache anymore."

The waiter reappeared, setting down huge ironstone platters heaped with plump, brown-freckled omelets oozing Gruyere, mounds of long, thin *frites* garnished with chopped parsley and wedges of grilled, oil-soaked sourdough smeared with sweet butter. He tried to slip away without making eye contact.

Cotton spoke right up. "*Monsieur, encore du vin, s'il vous plaît.*" The waiter nodded and rushed toward the kitchen.

"Crane, I wanted our first time to be—"

"It is. It will be. Right now I'm hungry. Just don't. Please."

Desperate, I wouldn't quit, and tried again. "What can I do to make this right?"

Cotton stopped just short of plunging a *frite* into his mouth. His long horse face looked sad, lost almost, but determined. Suddenly he winked wickedly. "Send me some Houseman. I bet he doesn't hang out in the library at Le Rosey."

"Smart ass."

"Educated ass, in any case, but likely to heal."

"You bird. Give me a break."

We both laughed.

Back at the hotel, along with the room key, the desk clerk handed me a telegram. The wire, sent from Wheelus, was dated the previous night, Friday, December 22, 1967.

LEAVE CANCELLED. CIRCUMSTANCES DICTATE
RETURN ASAP. WIRE AIRLINE AND FLIGHT. OPSTEIN.

I handed the wire to Cotton, reached for the phone and thought *What the fuck kind of shit has hit the fan now?* Settling down on the bed, I asked the hotel operator to try to connect me to Alitalia or TWA. After a single glance at the telegram and a similarly salty epithet, Cotton tried to wrest the phone from me with one hand and unbutton my jacket with the other.

I loved those hands. Like my own wrist and right hand, they were covered with burn scars. I pulled the boy into another hug, this one chaste. "Let me see about flights first, Crane. With Christmas, everything could be booked up."

"I hope so. Stay with me, Joe. Just today. I need that. Just today. Stay with me." Kissing my neck while I waited for an agent he whispered, "Not yet. Don't go yet."

Our streak of rotten luck held. The only Geneva-Tripoli connection before Tuesday was Alitalia through Rome, departing at six that evening. I checked my Bulova. It was past noon. I had packing to do.

"It won't be long, just until Easter," I said, releasing him, trying to get to my feet and return his kisses at the same time. "We can wait. Probably better that way. Probably we should have. You know?"

Cotton pulled me to him, kissing my mouth hard before shucking off his coat and sweater, kicking off his shoes, jumping up on the double bed and settling himself against the headboard. "Can I watch you pack, Hawk? You'll probably need to change clothes. All the way down to your Jockey shorts or less." Stretching out his long legs he wiggled the toes of his size fourteen feet. "Maybe we could take another shower together. Before you have to go."

"You're a very naughty boy," I said, laughing and pulling shirts and neckties out of the armoire, glad his good humor was restored. "I only keep you around because I love you so much."

"You'd better," Cotton replied, "because that goes double for me. You're my hero."

I was about to say, "And you are mine," when someone knocked on the door.

Without thinking, I opened it. A very tall, tanned, silver-haired man wearing what must have been a Savile Row suit and carrying a camel-hair overcoat looked me up and down. From the dissatisfied expression on his long thin face, I could tell I'd flunked some sort of test. "Is Cotton Boardman here?" he said.

"Papa? Aren't you supposed to be in Virginia?"

"Cotton?"

I took a step back and Winston Boardman swept past me.

"What are you doing here, son? Bunny and I went to your school, we wanted to pay you a surprise Christmas visit. They said you'd checked out for the day, to be with a friend. But when I called the number you'd left them, I got this cheap hotel."

Cotton was on his feet and playing defense in two seconds. Although he was an inch or two taller, they were obviously father and son. "Papa, this is Captain Joseph Decatur Harding from Ocala, Florida, and Vanderbilt University. He's the wing exec at Wheelus. He's my best friend. Mama likes him a lot. We play tennis. We swim."

Boardman looked me up and down a second time before turning his attention to the disordered bed and an untidy pile of linens beside the armoire: two pairs of briefs, a T-shirt, black socks, a blue broadcloth shirt and a towel.

"Do you? And does your Mama know you're here together in this—place?"

She almost undoubtedly did not, and Cotton was savvy enough to ignore the question. "I might not be anyplace if Joe hadn't put out the fire when I got burned. He got me to the hospital, even though he was burned, too. Mama made them give him a medal."

Cotton's thick, long hair was as disordered as the bed. His pale winter face was flushed pink with effort. He was defending the two of us like a samurai wielding an ancestral katana sword.

I was growing increasingly angry at being ignored, not to mention uneasy about what appeared to be Winston Boardman's well-founded suspicions. Cotton and I were buddies, mates. I couldn't let him fight this alone.

"If Cotton had known you were coming," I said, determined to cut through Boardman's studied rudeness, "we'd have hired a brass band."

"Irony is wasted on me, Captain," Boardman shot back. "So don't bother." He stared at the open bathroom door for a moment, taking in the heap of damp towels on the floor. "We appreciate everything you've done for Cotton, of course. Cotton's Mama, Lizzie, wrote me all about it. Or, rather, her second secretary did. Had I had my say, Cotton wouldn't have been in Libya at all. Far too dangerous a station for underage dependents. And he'd be with his mother right now. Or with Bunny and me in Charlottesville, going to Christmas parties."

Lizzie? That was new. I realized how little I knew about this rich, powerful family's dynamics.

Cotton struck back. "Papa, you must know Mama was recalled for talks. King Idris is unwell, the Black Prince unreliable. The last thing I wanted to do was haul ass across the pond to see a bunch of people I don't know or care anything about."

"They're your people, son, our friends. Not a bunch of small town bachelor officers, no matter how heroic." He looked at me straight for the first time. "No offense intended."

It has often been said that a gentleman is never unintentionally rude. Boardman clearly considered himself top drawer. For good measure he'd thrown in the deadly word *bachelor*. This was getting serious. How much did he know or suspect?

"Papa, actually it's none of your business what I do. You don't share custody. I'm almost eighteen. I can—"

Boardman, who hadn't even set down his overcoat, cut the boy off. "Put on your shoes and jacket, son. Bunny's at the hotel, the Palace. She'll be worried. We can call to your mother from there. You can stay with us until New Year's."

Cotton started to say something else. He looked like he was about to cry. He didn't move.

"Go with your father," I finally said. "I've got a train to catch. I have to pack. It was great seeing you, Crane. Merry Christmas."

"Goes double for me, Hawk. Times two. Happy New Year. See you at spring break."

I threw up the omelet, *frites*, toast, coffee, butter and jam on the train to Geneva. The Rome-Tripoli red-eye departed two hours late. I tried to sleep but didn't.

I was no fool; I knew my own IQ. My sex-drive was strong but generally under control. Having been abandoned by my father early on, I needed to be close to other males and yet seldom felt easy about it. Many such boys suffer through the bewildering surge of testosterone fever, however they may choose to act as grown men.

Months earlier, realizing I loved Cotton and admitting it to him, I'd vowed to make our first physical encounter an ecstatic one. Instead, I'd not only blown it, I'd endangered my career and put further meetings with Cotton at risk. For all I knew, I was being summoned back to Wheelus to face charges—depending on the evidence presented—for affairs with an enlisted Air Force medic, now in Southeast Asia; with an Army lieutenant, killed in battle in Vietnam, or my current once-a-week rubdown sessions with the Wheelus personnel chief, Major Hal Denman, a former prize-fighter. And that's not counting a night of very loose behavior at an oilman's all-male party in Tripoli the previous spring or my more-than-occasional visits to San Francisco's Embarcadero YMCA while stationed in California as a lieutenant.

A dozen snares could snap shut around my hairy ankle during the next few days. I might never leave Leavenworth alive. Cotton would be forced to marry a debutante.

About an hour out of Rome I got the shakes. Although the cabin was winter cold and I was wearing woolen blues, my crotch and armpits sweated up. I didn't smoke but considered begging a cigarette from one of the passengers in the smoking section, just to calm my nerves.

Alitalia served the prisoner-to-be a hearty breakfast: jailhouse coffee, hard roll and butter, apricot jam in a tiny jar and a foil-wrapped wedge of Laughing Cow cheese. I managed to get most of it down.

At Idris International Airport, Jeff was waiting outside customs and immigration. He looked like death. "It's bad," he said. "Worse than bad. We may both be eating dog turds instead of turkey. Merry Christmas, Captain Harding."

CHAPTER 3

EXTREME PREJUDICE

Ron Connolly must have tried to break his long, deadly fall. With better luck, he might have struck deep water instead of concrete. His left forearm had covered his face. The impact with the Uaddan Hotel's pool deck had splayed his knees and legs into a grotesque half-swastika shape. His right arm was thrown across his chest. He was wearing civvies: sport jacket, chinos and dark socks, but only one shoe. His back was to the police photographer's camera. His pretty Irish face was lost in shadow. It probably wasn't pretty any more.

"Pool boy found the body when he opened up," Jeff said. "The morning after you left, Joe. The Uaddan's fake minaret tower's balcony has got to be the equivalent of six, seven stories high."

We were meeting in Colonel Opstein's office. Jeff and I wore dress blues. Ops, in what must have been a nod to holiday informality, wore Levi's, workout boots and a Santa Claus T-shirt. Thick, dark hair did a three-sixty around the collar of the shirt. His oversize biceps stretched the shirt's sleeves tight. As usual, his scalp was buzzed, his face neatly shaved and he smelled faintly of Old Spice and clean sweat.

Jeff handed me another photograph, a saddle Oxford in close-up, the laces still tied. "Local authorities found this up on the balcony," he explained. "Matches the other; no question. Tower overlooks the pool deck but it ain't a straight shot down. Could be he took a dive on his own. But it sure does look like he put up a fight."

"And was pushed or thrown," Colonel Opstein added, for once stating the obvious. He was clearly disturbed, fighting to control his emotions. Losing one of your men to a killer or killers is about as tough as it gets, short of family. I know something about how it feels. Just before I arrived at Wheelus the previous year, the man slated to be my chief clerk had been sexually abused, viciously beaten and left to die on a roadside garbage heap. I helped settle his affairs and ship the body home.

"Must have been amateurs," I ventured. "Leaving the shoe behind like that."

Jeff handed me a third photo. "Keep going."

"If he was about to kill himself, why would he take off one shoe? And wouldn't professional killers collect any tell-tale evidence?"

"Shoe got knocked behind an old pigeon cage," Jeff said. "During the struggle, I bet. There's a light socket up there but the bulb was smashed."

The third photo, a close-up of Connolly's ruined face, was the hardest to take. His mouth was twisted open in a silent scream. From the angle of his head, I assumed his neck had been broken. I hadn't liked him much. As I said, he was nothing special: a paper-pushing draftee with a reserve commission. But he didn't deserve this. He had a wife, probably a big Irish family, buddies from school, maybe an old dog he still loved. My throat and ass clenched up tight. I started sweating again, worse than I had in the airplane. "He was a Catholic, sir. Probably didn't even have time to say a prayer."

The credenza behind Opstein was swathed in glitter paper and paved with ecumenical decorations: a plastic Christmas tree hung with blue stars of David, a hula-hula Santa in grass skirt and lei, Rudolph with a blinking red nose, and three or four battered packages that looked as if they started out as Bundles for Britain. Colonel Swanson was in Washington assisting Ambassador Boardman, leaving Ops as acting commander. No stickler for formalities, he'd decided to keep things low key and work from his own office rather than move to headquarters.

Jeff and I, on the other hand, were intent on observing military decorum in the face of potential disaster. The murder of an American officer on foreign soil could easily become an explosive international incident. Libya that winter was itself a political time bomb, with unrest, sabotage and rumors of thwarted *coups d'état* as common as battered Fiats. Ops and Jeff were extremely troubled and would no doubt grow more so as the details of Connolly's murder piled up. Despite my own three-day emotional roller-coaster ride, I hoped to calm the waters.

I couldn't have guessed how much worse it had gotten in the twenty-some hours since I received the wire from Ops. But what I expected to happen at that moment, just didn't.

A man was dead. We had a military checklist to follow. As Connolly's supervisor, Colonel Opstein would ordinarily serve as, or appoint, a custodian to collect and ship home Connolly's personal effects, safeguard any money on his person or in his American Express account, draft condolence letters to his family for the commander's signature and, most important, insure that the body was properly prepared, escorted home and rendered appropriate graveside honors. Because I had recent experience in such matters, and Ops had more important things to do, I figured that was why I'd been called back.

It was and it wasn't.

"We don't know what happened," Jeff said. "We may never know. Not only about how he died. We also didn't get to do no autopsy or lab tests. Connolly's body is gone, along with some shit from his office. We couldn't even go through his pockets."

"He's what?"

"On his way back to the States," Jeff continued. "Don't know how I'm gonna run any decent kind of investigation."

"Bunch of touch-and-go honchos arrived from Southeast Asia via Ankara," Ops put in. "Didn't bother reporting to me. Just started out trying to locate the OSI chief, Mr. Bivens, wanting permission to open up the boy's BOQ room. Bivens is in Tunisia for the holiday weekend. Word came back to me and I put a stop to it. The nerve. Burns my hairy butt."

"Who is—?"

"We'll get to that," Jeff answered. "Cool your jets. Took me five hours of feeding favors to the locals downtown just to get my hands on these pictures. Had to drink a lot of extra sweet mint tea because of the Christmas season and all. Call in a favor or two."

"You did good, Jeff-o," Ops said. "Best you could under the circumstances."

"See, Joe, the Uaddan people knew Connolly wasn't staying in the hotel. One look at his haircut and civvies and they spotted him for military. So they phoned my guard post right after they called the locals. Asked my sarge to get a-hold of me ASAP."

"You boys hang out at the Uaddan casino, that right?" As usual, Ops knew details about his men's off-duty affairs that they wished he didn't.

"I do like to gamble," Jeff admitted. "Calms my nerves. Joe drives the getaway car."

"He won eight hundred dollars playing blackjack one time," I added, bragging on my buddy's prowess with cards.

"You knew them and they knew you. Which is fine. Security's your job, son. You stay connected. Drink mint tea until your bladder gives out. I don't have to tell you that."

"No, sir," Jeff answered. "Let's say I've met the casino and hotel managers both, and was able to help them out a time or two as well."

"And they were looking at a very messy situation," Ops said, "and they hoped you could fix it for them."

Jeff turned to me. "Only I couldn't."

"Damnedest coincidence in the world," Ops said, turning to me.

I asked what had happened.

"Damnedest thing. If we assume that it *is* a coincidence. Here's what's happened. Like Jeff said, Connolly's remains and a few papers and personal effects from the motor pool are already on their way home. We had a C-130 drop in here unannounced four or five hours after Jeff's boys got the call from the Uaddan manager. Around noon, wasn't it? This airplane was en route from Southeast Asia to McGuire, New Jersey, with a couple dozen passengers. According to the flight plan, they were scheduled to refuel at Torrejon, up in Spain, and again at Goose Bay. But some kind of hydraulic leak developed, and so they put in here to check it out. Half my maintenance shop was on holiday leave and we had a heck of a time. You take it from there, Jeff."

"I identified the poor bastard, called for a military ambulance, had the medics transport him back here. Figured the flight surgeon would do an autopsy pronto, see if he was drunk or overdosed on drugs or maybe hurt real bad before he ever hit the deck. Once they took him, I started working the scene with the locals and hotel and casino staff—and turning up fucking nothing. You know how they are when there's trouble. Nobody saw or heard a thing. So I came on back here to brief the colonel."

Ops jumped back in. "The C-130 pilot finally reported to me about the same time. Told me some of his passengers had heard what'd happened from some of Jeff's troops—"

"Yes, sir, and I'm going to chew some ass over that. I tell the dumb fucks over and over, 'Use your ears and eyes, not your mouth, except to ask questions.'"

"The pilot informed me he just happened to have a mortuary team aboard. Said they were rotating back to the States after a year in country, and he volunteered to have them to take over handling the body. Save us the trouble."

"Which did have the benefit," Jeff pointed out, "of shipping out the corpse without the locals getting any more involved than they were. Customs, death certificate and what have you. But it wasn't right."

Connolly had presumably been killed in town and not on base so it was probably illegal and almost certainly against regulations and treaties to ship the body and any possessions before a custodian was appointed, responsibility handed over and a criminal investigation begun. There was no sense in saying so, so I didn't. Ops himself might eat shit for allowing such a plan. Only he hadn't allowed it.

Jeff's mouth twisted into a bad-cop snarl. "The colonel stated he'd have to think it over. Meanwhile the body-bag team did an end run on us, hunted down the flight surgeon at the hospital and talked him into giving up Connolly's remains. Come to find out he'd put off the autopsy until the day after Christmas. Said he wanted to enjoy his turkey dinner first. Body baggers didn't consult me or the colonel here—or the relevant regs. They just handed Doc a form to sign, he signed it, they produced a zip-up plastic garbage bag and, bam, they hauled poor Connolly over to their C-130 in one of the man's own vehicles."

A covered deuce-and-a-half-ton truck, I thought but didn't say. *For all we know, they took along a couple of cases of corned beef hash.*

Instead, I said, "We knew something funny was going on with Connolly—the off-the-books deliveries downtown, the no-names-games, and we brought that to you, sir. I'm pretty sure one of the men on the crashed Herc knew or recognized Connolly. But when I called him on it, not once but twice, he first denied it, then said he couldn't talk about it. He was being played like a hooked fish on a heavy line."

Ops didn't look happy. "And I served the fish to the old man and he said it didn't concern us, was strictly NATO business and already wrapped up."

"Only it wasn't," Jeff growled.

"I'm fucking well aware of that, son. What am I not aware of? What do you boys know you haven't told me yet? We got a dead man here."

"Only we don't, sir."

"Shit-can the jokes, Joe. Tell me why Connolly took emergency leave in late November? Will you tell me that? Jeff, you live with him. What was itching him?"

"He never said much. He brought work back to the BOQ in a briefcase. He hardly ever partied or had more than two beers. Went to Catholic mass. He made his bed up every morning, he kept his dresser top squared away, his shirts ironed. Joe calls him a bean-counter. Not having copies of the orders that we assume killed him, that must have worried him sick. Maybe he thought he saw a way to fix it."

"A filing clerk with gold bars," I said. "So yeah, lacking the paperwork must have figured in. Aside from the fact that we worked out together while you gentlemen jocked it up in the weight room, I barely knew him. Definitely, he was in over his head in some big way. I would agree he was trying to get help."

"And he went back to Chicago?"

Jeff and I looked at each other. "I don't know where he went," Jeff answered. "Like I said before, he didn't say much."

"Right," I answered. "He disappeared. A week or ten days later he was back, ready to jog around the track. That's all I know."

I was lying. It was far from all I knew. The carbon flimsies and photocopies of the wrecked Herc's flight plans and manifests were locked in my office safe, gilt-edged, get-out-of-jail cards that I wasn't ready to use. From what I knew so far, they might not even be relevant. I'd hand them over if events convinced me they made a difference.

I figured the session was done when Ops warned us to keep quiet about Connolly and said that if we turned up new information to let him know—him and him only. Always a pragmatist, Ops trusted the process up to a point, but he wanted to cover his bets.

So, as if it just entered his mind, he handed me a set of orders appointing me custodian of Connolly's personal effects. Jeff, who knew the lieutenant better, would head up a parallel investigation. His doing both would pose a conflict. And then Ops repeated what he'd just said in a slightly different way. Using his solemn rabbi voice and talking slowly, he said that, due to the unusual nature of the fatality and the unanswerable questions that might arise, everything we turned up should be run by him first. Everything. Assuming he liked what he saw and heard, it would next go to Colonel Swanson to be routed through USAFE to the Department of the Air Force. We should keep all of that in mind, he said, and do exactly as he ordered. It was a coded warning, one that took a while to figure out.

I trusted Ops and Jeff but there were too many loose ends here. I thought and thought again—and still didn't mention the papers in the safe. The murder could sneak around and bite me in the ass. Just like the crashed Herc had apparently gotten hold of Connolly's innocent butt.

Pete Ferrette, the late CIA station chief, had to be the link here. (I'd checked with the embassy; he'd reportedly suffered a fatal heart attack while on home leave.) But his career and death were mine fields I was wary of entering. As a presumably closeted gay man and a spy, he may have seen through my macho façade and passed the insight on. I hadn't told Ops I even knew him or suspected his inclinations, much less that he may have been murdered as the doomed plane rolled down the runway. Putting one dead man together with the other—figuratively, I mean—pretty much confirmed my hunch that the CIA or something like it was involved. Knowing that those guys played by their own set of rules, and didn't shrink from what was euphemistically called "termination with extreme prejudice," I wanted to stay well out of their way.

There was no doubt in my mind: Jeff and I had helped send a good, trusting man to his death. Our questions about irregular orders from unknown operatives concerning contraband ordinance and possible grand theft had triggered his request for emergency leave. Who had he talked to? What had he learned? If he'd mentioned our names and nosy questions to the agents that used him and presumably killed him, we were dog meat.

Sad, scared, guilt-ridden and bone tired after several nights and days on planes and in airports, I wanted to vomit again. The knowledge that I was withholding information from Ops and Jeff roiled my gut.

As soon as Ops ended the meeting, I ducked into a nearby latrine and lost the Alitalia breakfast. Merry Christmas, I thought bitterly, wondering as I doused my face with water how Cotton's family reunion was going. There was no way I could face turkey dinner at the chow hall, much less the O club. My beat-off buddy Hal Denman was on leave in Rome. His bishop in Detroit had arranged a ticket to Christmas mass at St. Peter's. He'd get to see the Pope.

So I did the only reasonable thing. I headed for the BOQ, stripped off my filthy clothes, showered, pulled on clean briefs and a T-shirt, fished a can of salted peanuts out of the dresser and opened a bottle of Spanish brandy. About halfway through the bottle I began writing a mushy, begging, contrite letter to Cotton. I had sense enough to tear it up and flush the pieces down the toilet a few minutes before I passed out cold.

CHAPTER 4

GHOSTS

I inventoried Ron Connolly's room a couple of days later. Airman Wilson assisted. Jeff observed and took notes. The saddest item in the lot was a Baltimore tract for Catholic married men entitled *Staying Pure When Away From Your Dear One.* Most of it read like a Boy Scouts manual or turn-of-the-century pamphlet on personal hygiene. Exercise, cold showers, prayer and Sunday mass were the four cornerstones of purity. Never give in to evil thoughts. Avoid occasions of sin such as dirty magazines, banned movies and loose women. When sexual temptation is greatest, pray to the Mother of God for strength. Self-control is a form of prayer and a sign of true masculine devotion. Offer it up.

Taking matters in hand was no more acceptable to the Church than to the Boy Scouts, in theory, anyhow.

Connolly's intentions may have been good but his practice was in line with the rest of us. I found two other handbooks hidden beneath a stack of neatly folded boxer shorts in the dresser, both consisting almost entirely of black and white photographs. The titles told the story: *Teenage Lesbian Nurses* and *Scandinavian Schoolgirl Sleepover.*

Jeff laughed out loud when he saw them. "I offered the man my fresh copy of *Playboy*, still in the wrapper, like a welcome-wagon present. He wouldn't touch it. Acted like I was some kind of weirdo."

Had Wilson not been there, I'd have answered, "Which you are, but not that

42

kind," and we'd have both laughed. Having shared a toilet for almost a year, we knew each other's kinks and habits, or most of them. Lesbian schoolgirls didn't figure in Jeff's fantasies. I knew that much.

Instead, I said, "The regs specifically direct the custodian to remove and destroy before shipment any items that might tend to cause embarrassment to the next of kin or reflect badly on the Air Force or the deceased. These puppies definitely qualify."

Wilson spoke right up. "I'll remove and destroy those objectionable items for you, Boss. Glad to do it. Unless you want to use—excuse me—destroy them yourself."

I handed them over. I doubted that Wilson had much of a sex life. "Actually, Airman, I prefer *The New Yorker* and *Esquire*. I have been known to glance at *Playboy* or *Hustler* once in a while. When I'm not reading Faulkner or Camus."

Wilson may have heard idle scuttlebutt concerning Captain Hard-on's off-duty pursuits. No use in confirming the rumors. Smoke screens are good. Let him wonder.

He slipped the magazines inside his blouse.

I continued the inventory: white T-shirts, black and white socks, running gear, jockstraps, uniforms, hats, caps, two prayer books, a history of the Chicago Fire, a paperback novel by Zane Gray, civvies shirts, pants and belts. And, half-hidden in Connolly's shaving kit, a three-pack of Sheik condoms. The orange-and-white box was familiar. My uncle Carl used the same brand and type, dry and lightly powdered with reservoir ends. When I was fifteen I'd tried one on for size. Although a tight fit, it felt so good I couldn't stop doing what I planned to do anyway. Later, I was afraid he'd notice that his new box of rubbers was one short. If he did, he didn't say anything.

Connolly's three-pack contained two. I handed the package to Jeff. "Mrs. Ron doesn't need to see these babies either. Airman, you've got your bedside reading. Captain Masters will dispose of these items at a later date."

Jeff threw me a funny look. He occasionally visited a downtown whorehouse run by an Italian woman. On Ops' orders, I drove him into town and waited in the madam's parlor while he did business. Alleys and narrow passageways in the old city were off limits after dark. Americans by themselves were always at risk. At Signora Agrigento's place, I never went upstairs. Jeff knew it. Wilson didn't need to.

Jeff tucked the box into his pocket. "Sometimes a man's got to take his shower wearing a raincoat. Safety first."

"Do you think Connolly took that kind of shower since he landed in Libya last summer?"

Jeff shrugged. "If he did, I'm not aware of it. We don't know what he did on leave—wherever he went. Let's hurry this up, OK?"

Jeff impounded a stack of letters, an address book and a calendar with cryptic notations on one or two dates each month.

There were also holy cards, a rosary and two framed studio pictures of Irish-American women, the mother and the wife. There was an eight-by-ten Christmas photo in a cardboard sleeve, probably shot the year before. Ron wore Air Force blues. His arms were wrapped around an adoring kid brother and his wife. There were parents, two grandmothers, three children and two women, obviously Ron's older sisters. One wore a Marine officer's dress uniform. The other was joined at the hip to an obese, balding Son o' the Sod. And, yes, in the bedside drawer, there was a snapshot of the teenage Ron with his arms around a hairy, happy mutt puppy in a backyard in what must have been Chicago.

You poor dumb bastard, I thought. *How the hell did you get yourself thrown off that tower?*

Watch your back, Captain Hard-on. You're in this mess up to your shoulder-boards. You and Jeff may not get out alive.

Drafting the condolence letters to Connolly's wife and parents was a bitch. Colonel Swanson knew the man only in the most formal sense. He told me he'd sign whatever I came up with. Aside from working out together, I didn't know Connolly much better. He did his job and got horny and lonely just like most single or unaccompanied men overseas. He was unwary enough to get himself used as a patsy and killed for what he knew. None of that belonged in letters to a grieving family. The tragic-but-unexplained-suicide angle wouldn't fly either.

Like any good desk-jockey, I kept a fat file of old correspondence for adaptation and reuse. Desperate, I pulled out the year-old letter to the parents of my murdered clerk-typist. It was a combination of parts of several form letters loaned to me by my body buddy, Major Denman. Bingo. Change the names and situations. Keep the narrative vague and brief. Use phrases like "terrible accident," "all efforts being made" and "an outstanding member of my command, an officer who will be sorely missed, a loss to us all, to the nation and, most of all, to you."

I ran the drafts by Ops, Jeff and Major Denman at Personnel. Airman Wilson typed the final versions on wing letterhead, with carbons for our files, and Colonel Swanson signed them. Rather than trust the letters to the post office and TWA, they went to the States in a courier's bag the first week of January. Connolly's personal effects, the clothing freshly laundered, followed a week later.

I hoped that was the last I'd hear of him or any other man dead under suspicious circumstances.

Major Erik Larsen, executive officer of the 155th Tactical Fighter Wing, stationed at Bitburg Air Base, West Germany, flew in for a pow-wow a week later. The wing had spent six weeks TDY at Wheelus the previous year, a stay that combined target and bombing practice over the desert with post-Vietnam decompression. During that period, on two different days, a pair of pilots, wingmen, bought the farm.

Although nothing was proved, there were rumors that the pilots, both of them married, had allowed their professional relationship to turn personal, perhaps even physical, while serving with distinction in Southeast Asia. Unwilling to face facts, or their wives, the guilty lovers flew their F-105Ds into the ground. I'd been involved in that mess, too.

Major Larsen was left with the unenviable task of drafting final reports on the loss of two expensive airplanes and two experienced pilots. He was also charged with helping his boss and their public information officer fend off repeated inquiries by both men's families, three congressmen, a senator, the Pentagon, *The Washington Post, Air Force Times, International Herald Tribune* and CBS.

We met in Colonel Opstein's conference room. Airman Wilson took shorthand notes and alternately played first one tape and then another. Larsen, having listened to the recordings of the second and last flight more than once, was fully aware that portions were missing. The missing minutes of tape—the machine had been wisely shut off by a protective flight controller—would have recorded my former wing commander addressing me as Captain Cocksucker and the wretched wingman accusing me of various sexual offenses and perversions, topping out at "queer as a three-dollar bill."

About ten minutes into the meeting, Larsen turned to me. "Captain, is it fair to say that you suspected some sort of alleged or possible homosexual component to these men's relationship and that you tried to give Lieutenant Totenberg an out?"

I didn't want any such thing said. Conroy, Totenberg and I had attended an all-male, anything-goes party in an oilman's downtown flat. Conroy and Totenberg didn't participate in the resulting orgy. They also didn't leave. I was told that the older man couldn't take his eyes off my naked butt. One or both of them might have described the scene later to anyone—a crew chief or another pilot, for instance. And Totenberg, unwound by grief, may have interpreted my subsequent, clumsy efforts at aid and comfort as coming on to him sexually.

I chose my words very carefully. "Major Conroy's death hit Lieutenant Totenberg very hard, sir. It would be fair to say that Major Conroy was his role model and hero. After you cut him loose—" the 155th had left Totenberg in Wheelus hospital when they departed for Bitburg "—he was desperate. I tried to counsel him. He'd hit bottom. He needed a friend."

Larsen glanced at Ops. "We have priests and doctors for that, as I recall."

Ops knew the story, or most of it. "The man didn't trust them, Major, and I believe rightly so. He talked to Joe some. He talked to one of the nurses. Then he tried to put the make on her. She told him where he could shove it."

Larsen looked at me. "He didn't suggest that you—-"

"Of course not, sir."

"Son, have you been to Nam yet?"

"No, sir. I put in for it and got sent here instead."

"Nam's a city, Saigon, surrounded by jungles and cesspools and razor wire in every direction. Half the gooks want to kill you, the other half want to sell you their sister. It makes some men go nuts, do things they'd never do back in civilization. You get my drift?"

"Yes, sir."

"So let me ask you a different way. Do you think it's possible that the major and the lieutenant, you know, got the crazy hornies, maybe smoked some dope, got accidentally intimate, broke the regs and paid the price for it?"

"Sir, I truly don't know what those two men did together or felt for each other. I don't know why they crashed their airplanes. It's not my business to have an opinion. Sir."

"Do you believe it was intentional?"

Ops cut me off, basically ending the conference. "Major, what we know is that the manufacturer, Republic Aviation, says both those pilots had their afterburners kicked in when they hit the ground. The airplanes were in good order. It wasn't any accidents."

Ops's pragmatism had surfaced. He went by the book and did whatever it took to get the mission accomplished. He also wanted to distance me from further involvement in the investigation.

"Joe saved one of my planes and pilots," he continued. "He made a hell of an effort to talk Totenberg down. We did everything we could to save him. And we came up short. Unfortunately, Major, nobody's ever going to know why those pilots killed themselves. Whatever made them do it, they took their reasons to the grave."

That wasn't quite true. The sex orgy was fact. Conroy, Totenberg or any number of guests might have described my behavior that night—or been affected by the sight of horny, naked, drunken men doing what we'd been doing. At least two others, non-participants, know all about it. But one was serving time in a Libyan jail for murder. The other was in Southeast Asia. He loved me and wasn't likely to talk.

Larsen returned to Germany. Ops probably didn't give it a second thought. I hardly slept for the next three nights.

On January thirty-first, during a lunar new year truce, Viet Cong insurgents and North Vietnamese soldiers attacked strategic towns, villages and bases all across South Vietnam. The ancient capital of Hue was captured. More than six thousand civilians were killed in that city alone. Part of the American embassy in Saigon was also seized, though soon freed. Eventually, our side—if only temporarily—did regain control of the south. But American and allied casualties were high and a turning point had been reached.

News of the Tet disasters came in bit by grisly bit. We'd thought we were winning hearts and minds. We'd believed the Army generals, the secretary of defense and President Johnson when they solemnly swore that progress was being made, that pacification was working, that the light at the end of the tunnel was not the Ho Chi Minh Express headed in our direction. Since then, of course, we've learned that none of them took seriously the dispatches of reporters on the ground or the enemy troop estimates by CIA experts. What the administration told the public up to that point was mostly lies, damn lies and artfully fudged statistics.

I'd had a hand in the involuntary transfer of three men from Wheelus to Southeast Asia the previous year. Two were among the known dead that first week. Both were bad actors, a doctor and a pharmacy clerk who endangered lives. Both were reassigned to a triage unit near the demilitarized zone. When the DMZ was overrun, the unit was wiped out. After I heard the news, I laid a twenty-four-hour Oh-Shit trip on myself. I was a killer, I felt. I'd helped send men to their graves. Though they'd deserved a taste of endangerment, they paid too dearly for serious misbehavior. I got over it fast, however. If it hadn't been them, I rationalized, other innocent or at least less guilty troops would have taken their places.

I heard nothing about the third man, a tech sergeant, also a medic and a truly good man with whom I'd had a brief affair. The match didn't work out, mostly because of my growing friendship with Cotton. The now-dead DMZ duo had been about to expose the sergeant and me as queers. Had they succeeded, we'd have been charged with conduct unbecoming, serial sodomy, the whole dirty laundry list. We'd have been busted, maybe jailed. I had no choice. I used connections to send Sergeant Duane Haynes as far away as possible. A clinic at Udorn Air Base, Laos, seemed a much safer place for him than an OSI interrogation room. When the news from Vietnam got worse and then terrible, Duane stayed on my mind.

Major Hal Denman, the personnel chief, had been my accomplice in shipping Duane and the two assholes to Southeast Asia. His mentor, rising brigadier Elmo McAddams, like Hal a grounded flyer, worked at the Pentagon in Air Force personnel. He knew which strings to pull. Hal would ask the general to check on Duane if I said the word. But I decided to wait. What was going to happen, would happen. I'd done what I could do to protect him. Instead, after several days of worry, I caught up with Hal in the chow hall. I figured the subject might come up anyway. It did.

Hal and I got together every week or so to trade rubdowns. We would drink Spanish brandy in his BOQ suite, slowly strip each other, massage each other's backs and fool around like high school boys. Hal was bald, well built, didn't smoke and had very shapely ears. It relieved the pressure without a lot of drama. He was committed to General McAddams. I had Cotton, although Hal knew little about him. Hal and I weren't lovers, we were buddies—buddies who enjoyed taking care of each other.

We didn't have a set night to get off. One of us would make a phone call or drop by the other's office at quitting time. We rarely missed Friday happy hour. Somehow, the date would be made.

Harold Patrick Denman had attended parish schools in suburban Detroit. He was an only child with no dad. A shy kid with a slide rule, he got beaten up by bigger boys until an older cousin showed him a few defensive moves. One thing led to another: a downtown gym, a boxing coach, the Golden Gloves, the nickname One-Punch, a college scholarship, ROTC training, navigator's wings and a married pilot named McAddams. He kept fighting through all of it, right up to the inter-service finals. He won his weight class, putting an enlisted Marine on the deck, and retired from the ring. Soon after that, he failed a hearing test and was grounded. He'd taken one too many punches, he told me sadly, and more than once.

He kept a signed, framed photograph of his hero, Rocky Marciano, in his quarters. When we got together that February night, we started out, as we usually did, sitting on the big leather couch he owned, drinking brandy and facing the portrait of Rocky, getting a load off our minds. Sometimes we ended up on the handmade carpet, other times in bed.

"The news, it's all bad," he said, pouring us a second drink. He was wearing trunks, thick white cotton socks and, in a nod to the Mediterranean winter, an Air Force blue sweatshirt. Although I was six or seven inches taller, we probably weighed about the same. We were both in good shape and needed this sort of outlet.

"You heard about—?" I said, meaning the men we'd sent to the DMZ.

"Real bad news for them. Tough titty, though. Abused drugs, abused women, put you through the wringer. The world is better off without the bastards."

"I'll drink to that."

Hal rubbed the top of my crew cut head. "Are you worried about your sergeant, Duane What's-his-name?"

"Sure. A little."

"You already had one friend killed over there, what was his name, the Army lieutenant, Hawaiian?"

"Kim. Kim Nakamura. Huh. I hadn't thought about him in, oh, you know, days. Since this started, Tet." Suddenly, I was back in California, in a cheap motel. Kim was dancing a male hula for me. He had an all-over tan, skin like honey, almond eyes, boundless sweetness. "He got shipped over there by mistake."

"I remember. A jealous superior officer, had a wife, stepped on his own pecker, big time."

"His and Kim's."

Being gay had never seemed like a curse to me. I took reasonable risks and got what I wanted most of the time. I couldn't figure out why male-male relations so often led to trouble.

Hal patted my thigh gently, moved his hand slowly up and down and patted me again. "You know, Joe. I like this."

"What, my leg? My chinos?" I covered his hand with mine.

"Yeah, sure. What I mean, though, you and me. We get along, no pressure, just good times. Do what we like to. Secrets stay safe. No questions asked."

"We're two lucky guys, Rocky. As long as our luck holds."

Hal seemed to change the subject, but actually he didn't. "Got a call from Elmo today. He used a secure scramble phone, so we could talk some."

That sounded like trouble. I kept it neutral. "Is the general OK?"

"He's got a bug up his ass about Ron Connolly. Wanted to know what kind of shit has hit the rumor-mill fan over here. You know, beyond shock and surprise. Sounds like the family's not satisfied with what they been told. I said I'd ask you."

"You saw the letters I drafted for the old man."

"I saw two pieces of Naugahyde butt cover."

I didn't want to lie to Hal but I sure couldn't tell him all I knew. Knowing half of what'd happened to Connolly would put him in danger. So I covered my butt with the reg book. "The old man appointed me Ron's custodian. The regs don't allow me to reveal anything connected to the case. Everything has to stay confidential."

"The case? OK, that clears up one question we had."

"His death. I shouldn't have said case. I'd better shut up. You get me drunk and I'll say anything."

Hal squeezed my thigh, meaning 'Don't give me that shit.' "Regs don't allow me to touch you like this. Or allow you to let me. But you do. I do."

Hal was strong. I got the message. "I want you to. This is complicated. Colonel Opstein specifically ordered me—"

"Ops? Not Swanson?"

Maybe I was a little too drunk. "I shouldn't have said that either."

"OK, Joe. We'll drop it. One more thing, though. Elmo added a heads-up. Said to tell you an off-line investigator is on the way over."

Oh, shit. I hated lying to Hal. I was in love with Cotton and felt halfway guilty about using Hal as a sexual substitute. He'd told me about loving Elmo McAddams and I wanted to tell him about my boy. But I was scared to. The whole affair might explode. Winston Boardman had sounded angry as well as vindictive. A man-boy scandal. If Hal knew about it and didn't report it, he could go down with me.

Trouble. Minutes earlier I'd silently celebrated this male-male relationship as trouble free. Now it wasn't. I should have done the decent thing: walked out and never come back. But I was in too deep with Hal. I could neither explain my dilemma nor break off whatever it was we had.

So I did what I could to satisfy Hal and assuage my own guilt. I put my hand on the ex-prize-fighter's muscular shoulder and whispered, "How about a nice rubdown, Rocky? You ready for that?"

He said what I wanted to hear. "Fuckin'-A, Joe. I could use a nice rubdown." He put his hand on my belt buckle. "I bet you could use one, too. And old One-Punch is just the guy to do it."

A couple of days later, Jeff stopped me in the locker room. "Let's go to the souk," he said without preliminaries. "The old town. What about tonight?"

"You want to buy a rug?" I knew what he wanted and he knew I knew it. Clearly he was tired of dating the *Playboy* centerfold.

"Signora's place. You drive me, like Ops said. I buy you a steak dinner at the club."

"Last I heard, Ops told you to quit it."

Jeff scowled, turned away, faced me again. "OK, dinner with real Italian wine at the Swan restaurant."

"Now you're talking." I punched his arm. "You know I'm joking. About the Swan, I mean. Whatever you need. Tonight's wide open."

"Let's go shower," Jeff said. "The Swan it is. But on one condition."

"Namely?"

"You think about giving one or two of Signora Agrigento's girls a test drive. They're pros—nothing like your stuck-up sorority girls in college. You don't know what you're missing."

Yes, I did. But I went along. "You could be right. Maybe sometime. Not tonight. I have a headache."

After a double-take, he laughed. "You're a card, Joe. OK, tell you what. I've got a new *Playboy* back in the room. Just turned up in today's mail. You can check it out while you wait in the signora's parlor. Might give you a few ideas. You won't be able to help yourself."

We had to park a couple of blocks from the whorehouse. I tipped a kid a buck to watch the Pontiac, told him I'd double it if he kept the car safe.

Passing through the shadowy souk, we saw a tall man turn a corner ahead of us, heading away from the madam's. He looked familiar, at least from the back—gray crew cut, spine like it was tied to a rail, marching rather than walking.

"Was that the old man?" I whispered.

"Swanson? Might've been. He's divorced, right? Is he dating anybody?"

I said I didn't know, had never thought about it.

We reached the door of the house. Jeff rang the bell. "Colonels get blue balls, Joe. Just like the rest of us. It's none of our business, anyway. So forget it."

The door opened. Forget it was the last thing I'd do. If Swanson was plugging Signora Agrigento's girls, I might have just picked up another Monopoly card.

Off duty, Jeff wore motorcycle boots and leather wrist cuffs. He liked discipline, sometimes even needed it to get off. He'd reluctantly explained the situation after a cheap whore hurt him and I covered for him. He'd learned about leather in a Colorado bunkhouse one summer during college. That girl was a biker slut. Signora Agrigento employed a dominatrix with a much more professional touch. The madam led Jeff upstairs as soon the door closed behind us.

I settled down on a couch in the waiting room and opened the new *Playboy*. An old woman brought me a small glass of Amaretto and set it on a low table beside me. After a few minutes, the madam returned. I asked her to sit and she did so, clapping her hands once. The servant reappeared, this time with mint tea, two small plates and a hammered brass tray of Italian pastries.

I couldn't decide between the cream horns and the Sicilian nun's breasts so I took one of each. The signora smiled. "At your service, Captain. I am so happy you catch my little jokes."

"You take care of my friend, Signora."

"It is my pleasure, Captain. Now, what can I do for you?"

I asked if an American had been in the house earlier. "Gray hair, good figure, almost as tall as me, fifty or so."

She took a sip of tea and stared at me as if I were a choir boy. "I never discuss my visitors, Captain. It would not be fair. Or good business. It's out of the question. You understand my position?"

The signora might have been somebody's grandmother. She was well dressed and elegantly coiffed, she spoke good English and clearly knew her trade.

I pushed. She didn't budge. Finally she smiled and said, "You know, Captain, my girls are clean. Two or three might be called beautiful."

I said I was sure she was right.

"My servant pours you drinks. I offer you sweets. That, too, is good business."

I nodded and sipped.

"You sit in my parlor and read this—" she gestured at the magazine "—this literature when you could be taking your pleasure."

I was about to answer but she held up her manicured hand. "It is possible, Captain, that on occasion I introduce a particular client to a clean, well-behaved boy. Yes, I have done that."

She had my number all right. "I don't want a boy," I answered, lying through my teeth.

"No? Well, I also have access—it that the right word? Hmm, so to say, not a few of my visitors have taken their pleasure with a local man of my close acquaintance. He is of your age, maybe a bit older. He does not understand English but he thoroughly understands how to satisfy certain men's needs. Perhaps you spend an agreeable hour with him—as with the person you seem to imagine visited us earlier? And no one would know. Not even—especially—your friend upstairs. You see?"

Surely Colonel Swanson wasn't amusing himself with rent boys. If he was, maybe I'd won a stack of cards.

I used a dodge that had worked before. "Signora, do you honestly believe I'm not tempted by your beautiful girls? Do you think I'm not jealous of what your visitors do here? If I wanted a clean boy or a willing man I could find plenty at Wheelus, that's for sure. But, no, you don't understand. I've taken Jesus as my personal savior. When He called me, I went down on my knees and made a vow to Him. I promised to save myself for the woman I marry. To be as virginal as my bride. It's in the Bible."

Signora Agrigento patted my knee and winked. "That's in the American Bible, Captain. There you must behave. Here is different. According to local custom, you could certainly marry one of my girls tonight and legally divorce her tomorrow. With a snap of your fingers. Just as she could divorce you."

Beaten, I said I'd keep it in mind.

On the way back to the base Jeff turned moody and angry. He refused to speculate further about Colonel Swanson. "Everybody's got secrets, Joe. You should know that better'n anybody. Forget about it, OK? Mind your own business."

Secrets. The madam had easily nailed me. I wasn't one of her customers and she owed me neither discretion nor silence. She could whisper, demand money, anything. She could even tell Swanson that a very tall, slim, nosy young officer had spotted him leaving, was asking about him, and that the officer was not remotely interested in her girls' services. She could suggest, infer, probably even provide my name.

I had no Monopoly card for that. My questions had gained me nothing and only made me more vulnerable. The Swan restaurant's expensive pasta and vino were lead in my gut.

Maybe I should I screw one of the signora's girls, just to prove I can do it. I've done it before.

The clean, well-behaved local boy would be easier, Joe. More fun and probably less expensive. The signora wouldn't care as long as she got her fee. Right?

You really are nuts, aren't you? Maybe it's time Jeff found himself a new chauffeur. Stay home and beat off with old One-Punch. No risk in that.

Once Cotton's eighteen it'll all be OK.

Sure it will, Joe. If you don't get arrested first.

CHAPTER 5

A COUPLE OF PIECES OF CAKE

Colonel Mark Earl Swanson's thin, straight nose was set high on his face. His jaw jutted out like the prow of a dreadnaught. Otherwise, he wasn't bad looking. His body was slim but solid, his back straight as a cadet's, his height a couple of inches short of mine. His uniforms, even his flight suits, were always freshly pressed. I figured his boxers were probably starched and ironed as well. Divorced, with college-age kids, he lived off base, by himself as far as I knew, and was looked after by a local couple. I'd been to his villa only once, on a weekend, delivering classified documents that required his endorsement ASAP. He didn't ask me inside. The opposite of warm and fuzzy, he kept all his officers at a distance the first couple of months he was in country.

Which was fine with me. I'd grown too close to the man he succeeded and gotten burned, literally and figuratively.

Prior to arriving at Wheelus, Swanson had been in Washington for a year, as vice-chair of the USAF Office of Special Projects, whatever that might be. The eighteen months prior to that he was vice-wing commander at Anderson Air Base, Guam.

I was determined to win him over by sheer administrative efficiency. Under my direction, the paperwork flowed like the mighty Mississippi. Reports and memos arrived on his desk at precisely the moment they should, neither a day early nor a minute late. Classified communications and directives, reg books and phone trees stayed current and were kept close at hand. Officers scheduled to be promoted, interviewed or chewed out received polite phone calls one day ahead, reminding them of the appointment. Staff meeting agendas, drafted by Colonel Opstein and myself, were correctly typed and neatly mimeographed by Airman Wilson.

My first real break came when Colonel Swanson discovered a stack of officers' performance reports stashed inside the 1966 wing scrapbook in the bottom drawer of his desk. They'd been prepared months earlier, for the previous commander's signature, and left unendorsed and unsigned after he shipped out. Swanson's thumb punched the call button on his desk and stayed there.

When I got to him he was on his feet, his normally tan face flushed. "Promotions and careers depend on these documents moving forward, Harding. Shouldn't they have been held in your suspense file? And be in Washington by now? I don't know half these men. Some have rotated out, is that correct?"

I ruffled through the papers. A couple of names jumped up. One was the abusive flight surgeon who'd died at the DMZ. "I'll have to take full responsibility, Colonel. These never crossed my desk, but they should have. It's my office. I'll fix it."

"How can you fix it? I can't write endorsements on people I've never met."

"Give me two days, Colonel. Records can be reconstructed. We can ship them direct to Washington. I have a contact in the Pentagon. The pipeline from personnel through USAFE does get log-jammed, so I'd better get to work."

"Two days, Harding. Or I'll know the reason why."

Four minutes later, Airman Wilson and I presented ourselves to Major Denman. Ignoring the fact that his office should have contacted me about the missing documents, I explained the situation, ending respectfully with, "Sir, we have to be creative."

"Creative? These are official records. We can't just make them up."

"Yes we can. It's boilerplate. You've got clerks who can draft endorsements in their sleep. Wilson will type them up for the old man's signature. Or do you think we ought to post-date them to the week after the *old* old man flew out?"

"Joe! We can't do this. People will know."

"They may know. But there will be no complaints, I can almost guarantee it. We will use some very advanced administrative methods developed in Fifteenth Air Force."

"Explain."

"Every officer will be rated no lower than extremely-well-qualified. He or she will be cited for solid achievements, levels of efficiency and readiness substantially above his or her peers, a high state of motivation, outstanding initiative and qualities of leadership that should be rewarded with promotion at the earliest possible opportunity."

"Jesus Christ, Joe. Are you nuts?"

"Except for Doc Gelber. Hammer his ass to the cross."

"Jesus, Mary and Joseph. We—"

I cut off that line of lamentation. "With all due respect, Major, I would suggest that you ask your clerks to vary the language as much as possible."

"We'll never get away with it."

"The colonel ordered me to fix this. It will work. Sir."

It did. On Friday, I opened a happy hour-to-midnight tab for Denman's enlisted staff at the NCO club. On Saturday afternoon, the major and I began our weekly workout with a fresh bottle of Spanish brandy.

The second break was Dottie Bacon, Airman Second Class, a jiggely-jugs Daisy Mae from Dallas, Texas. Her uniforms were like a second skin. She was also a good typist and no fool. Airman Wilson brought her to my attention just before Christmas. She'd been wasting her talents in the commissary office. She was happy to move up the food chain.

She began work at headquarters the first Monday of 1968. Colonel Swanson hadn't returned from Washington so we had a few days to get the team organized. Wilson and I put her through her paces: filing, shorthand from dictation, mimeograph, inter-office and command mail, in and out boxes and, most important, telephone and front office etiquette. Ambassadors, generals and local poobahs called and visited headquarters almost as often as officers and airmen. Messages had to be correctly noted and calls properly directed. Dottie was especially good at welcoming middle-aged men to the office.

"Why Major," (or whatever the title), she'd gush. "Welcome to the headquarters of the best little flying training wing in the *world*. The colonel, he's gonna be with you in just two shakes of a little lamb's *tail*."

There was seldom any doubt which lamb's tail such visitors would like to shake.

Airman Bacon wasn't tall. To compensate, she wore heels that were probably higher than regulations permitted. I didn't call her on it and neither did the colonel, ordinarily a stickler for dress codes. He and I were both tall and trim. Wilson was average except in the waistline department. Beside us, in oxfords, Bacon seemed almost dwarf-like. OK, a very pretty dwarf with an hour-glass figure and a sultry Texas drawl.

Airman Bacon wasn't cleared for top secret but that turned out not to matter. She was highly competent at buttering up the divorced, studly Swanson.

"Very intelligent girl," he remarked a month or so after he returned from the States. "Hard worker, too."

Works to make you hard, I thought but naturally didn't say. Airman Buster Wilson wasn't immune, either. One morning, returning to my desk from the colonel's private office, I came upon him leaning over Bacon's shoulder, reading a document. His pants were tented out by a very inappropriate erection.

"Airman Wilson," I said as if unaware of anything at all. "Why don't you take early lunch?"

He forced the thing down with both hands, snatched up his cap and duck-walked quickly out of the room.

Airman Bacon grinned at me and winked. "You men. I don't know how we get any work done around here at *all*. I may have to get a fire hose after that boy one day."

He'd fire-hose you in a minute, baby, I thought but again didn't say. "It's tough being a single man at Wheelus," I answered genially. "So few single women around, and especially so few single, attractive women."

"You includin' me in that category, I hope, Captain?"

Gotcha, girl.

"Oh, absolutely. But we have to keep it off the record, OK?"

Buster Wilson, for all his skills, was no whiz at taking dictation. The colonel was several pay grades above drafting his own documents. Bacon scored a home run here. Within the first month, I noticed that more and more of the colonel's unclassified memos and correspondence were being dictated to Bacon rather than drafted by me. I also noticed, but didn't put too much thought into the fact that Airman Bacon, pencil and steno pad in hand, occasionally entered the colonel's private office and closed the door behind her.

Like most men of his generation and type, Colonel Swanson took for granted a limitless sense of entitlement as a white, Christian, heterosexual male, subspecies *Americanus militariensis*. Had Bacon or Wilson or I cracked a farting-priest or jerk-off joke in his presence he'd have been shocked, maybe angered. Yet he seemed to think we enjoyed being treated to off-color remarks about Martin Luther

King, Jr., Joan Baez, dope-sniffing hippies, farmers' daughters caught with their drawers down and, worst of all, fairies, queer homos and fruits with nuts.

"A man walked into a bar in Greenwich Village," he might start out. "And he didn't see any women—"

I let it slide because that was what gay men and women in the military had to do. Wilson laughed and played along, probably imagining that some sort of macho bonding was going on. Bacon tossed it back at the colonel indirectly.

Following a staff meeting, for instance, after all the other participants had saluted goodbye, the four of us were standing around the outer office chatting, basically waiting for quitting time. Buster, looking Dottie up and down and joke-ogling her tight uniform and ample bustline, remarked that he didn't know how he was going to do any more typing or filing that day anyway, and he hoped she'd help him out.

Dottie put her hands on her hips, Annie Oakley in blues. "There must be some dumb gal on base that'll take pity on your little dill pickle." And with this she held up her dainty right hand, thumb against fingertips, pumping the magic ring. "But it sure ain't me."

Wilson looked shocked. Had he never gotten a hand job from another human being?

"No, not this gal. She don't ever fool around with horny airmen, not her. Not *ever*." Then she slapped her hands together and tick-tocked her hips, Mae West-style. "Now, the captain here. That would be another matter."

Even the colonel laughed.

Humor like this could cut two ways. I put an end to it by acting as if I agreed. "Fraternization, Airman Bacon. Strictly against the regs. The temptation is hard to resist. But I believe I'd rather keep my commission."

I'd paraphrased Oscar Wilde and nobody caught it. Butter wouldn't melt in my mouth. I took stupid risks for nothing.

CHAPTER 6

CLICK, CLICK, SWAGGER STICK

L ieutenant Ron Connolly's older sister, Major Rae Connolly, USMC, appeared at headquarters a few days after Major Eric Larsen departed. The lady Marine was the off-line investigator General McAddams had warned us about. She was tough.

Protocol required that she ask permission to use facilities on base, including the O club and exchange. It was no different than a sailor boarding a warship. She didn't have to report to me, but the brigadier had given her my name, rank and position as primary contact. Colonel Swanson was in his office and so, after thirty seconds of small talk, I showed her in and introduced them. She cut him a proper salute and they shook hands. He smiled. She didn't.

She was as tall as her brother, bone thin, with few curves and almost no butt. Even standing at ease, she looked like she was braced. Despite having flown coach from Washington via Madrid on TWA overnight, her creases were sharp and her uniform wrinkle-free. She had her brother's dark hair, fair skin and Irish face and eyes. Even the straightest guy in the locker room would have agreed that Ron was the prettier of the two.

"I hope you don't mind, Colonel. We just don't understand. We're still in shock over this. Eileen—that's my sister-in-law, Ron's wife, widow rather—Eileen is especially disturbed. I was granted a week's compassionate leave to settle family affairs. Talking to Ron's buddies here, like Captain Harding, maybe that will make a difference. And going over the ground."

I've already said that her brother and I were workout partners, not close friends. But there was no reason to contradict her in front of the old man.

Swanson told her to depend upon him for anything she needed. His tone was gracious, almost fatherly. "I don't think any of us understand what happened, Major. Your brother's unfortunate death hit us all very hard." He nodded at me. "Joe, you know, was custodian of his personal effects."

She threw me a pointed look. "You were? I was not aware of that fact."

I'd signed the property list and several other forms. Maybe she hadn't seen them.

"So I'll want to talk to you, Captain. Whenever you have the time."

Swanson waved his hand. "Take off, Joe. Glad to meet you, Major. Anything I can do, Joe will take care of it."

Oh, thanks, Colonel. Even though the major's arrival was highly unusual, indeed inappropriate, I figured Swanson was cutting her plenty of slack because she was military and female and her sibling had served under him. Her presence clearly implied she was checking up on us. He didn't seem to mind.

We were hardly out of the building when she said, "You were the custodian so you must have drafted those letters. Is that right, Captain."

"Call me Joe, Major."

"Captain will do for the moment. You did draft them?"

"Yes, ma'am. I did."

"How could you do such a thing? My mother may never get over what you wrote. Daddy fought in World War Two, in the Navy. Tell me, Captain. What the hell were you thinking?"

"Now I'm the one who doesn't understand, ma'am."

"How many military condolence letters have you seen, Captain?"

"Not many. A few."

"I thought so. I've seen dozens. I've written them. I've never read anything as cruel as what was sent to mama and Eileen over that man's signature."

We were walking toward Jeff's station house. I halted, said, "Ma'am, hold up. Here's what I did. I went out of my way to be as vague and sympathetic as possible. Because we didn't know what happened, or why. Colonel Opstein, the acting wing commander at the time, Captain Masters, the top cop, and Major Denman, Personnel chief, they all signed off on those letters."

"Why didn't you know? What kind of half-assed investigation did your brig chaser run? And the local authorities?"

She'd put me on the defensive and I was fighting blind. I knew more than it seemed safe to say, and yet she was accusing me of intentional cruelty when I'd gone as far as possible in the opposite direction.

"Do you have copies of those letters, ma'am?"

"Of course I do." Reaching into the canvas briefcase she carried, she pulled out a manila file, extracted two photocopies and handed them to me.

A glance at the letters told me we had another problem. "This is all wrong, ma'am."

"You bet it is, Captain. And I want some answers."

"I mean this isn't what I drafted or had my clerk type up. These are not what Colonel Swanson signed. They're on our letterhead but they don't have signatures."

She retrieved the photocopies and scanned them. "I hadn't noticed that."

The texts themselves were ball-chillers. "Cruel" didn't cover it. Whoever composed the letters stated that Lieutenant Connolly had been drinking heavily and alone in the Uaddan Casino bar, somehow found his way upstairs and either lost his footing in the dark or intentionally took his own life by jumping off the minaret's balcony. An autopsy, the letters went on to say, reported high levels of alcohol in his blood and needle marks in his arms. The letter also stated that "in all probability" the death benefit and G.I. life insurance would eventually be paid and the possibility of suicide dismissed.

I had drafted none of this. "First of all, ma'am, no autopsy was performed at Wheelus Hospital or at the Royal Hospital in Tripoli. That I know for sure."

"Tell me why I should care where it was performed."

"If, Major. If it ever happened."

Major Connolly glared at me. "Why are you doing this, Captain?"

"Because you've just thrown a grenade under my desk. I don't like being fragged."

"Were you here when he—that night?"

"No, ma'am. I was in Switzerland."

"And Colonel Swanson?"

"Washington, I believe."

"But, as custodian, you did oversee the preparation and shipment of my brother's body?"

"No, ma'am. He was picked up by a mortuary team that happened to be passing through. Their plane broke down and took a day to fix. His remains were flown to the States before I could get back. You didn't know that?"

She didn't answer for maybe thirty seconds. Then her Marine drill instructor façade kicked back in. "This is a rotten can of worms, Captain. This stinks to high heaven. I'm not believing any of it."

"Yes, ma'am. It sure the hell is—and does."

It suddenly looked like we might get along. "Let's go see Jeff," I said. "The top cop. Your little brother's toilet mate."

Jeff, with his taste for dominant women, handled the major much better than I had. "You look just like him," he said after the two had shaken hands in his office. "An Irish rose from the old sod of Chicago."

She nodded but didn't smile at the compliment. "Roses have thorns, Captain. I'm not here to make nice and I don't have a lot of time for chit-chat." She reopened the briefcase and handed Jeff the photocopies. "I promised my daddy I'd get to the bottom of this. Take a look at these, if you will."

Jeff scanned first one, then the other, and looked up at me, his face a question mark. "You didn't write these, Joe. Or at least it's not what you showed me."

"That's what I told the major."

"I'd come back from hell to kill a bastard that sent this kind of bullshit garbage to my wife or mama."

"All right, gentlemen, now that I know these are fakes, I need help finding the bastard who made the switch. I'll take him down personally. But that's a mere detail. I need to know how and why my brother died."

Jeff held up his hands. "We don't know, ma'am."

"Are you guys reading off the same script?"

Jeff rechecked one of the letters. "Your brother was a two-beer man, if that. At least since I met him. And I know what he looked like without any clothes on. He didn't have no needle tracks on his arms, not the last time I saw him."

"Which was when?"

"A day or two before what happened."

"Go on, Captain."

"You sure he didn't get no bad news, Major? Debts he couldn't pay? Wife trouble? Or have a habit of getting depressed and drunk around the holidays?"

"He was an altar boy. I never even heard him swear. His wife loved him. We all did. But I do know there was something bothering him."

"What's that, ma'am?"

She seemed lost for a moment. "We're Catholics. Catholics don't kill themselves like this. Liquor, maybe, but—"

"So what was it, ma'am?"

"I believe it would be useful to talk to the people who found him, last saw him—after you did, I mean. Talk to them first, to level the field a bit. The local police were called, I presume?"

"Yes, ma'am. The hotel spotted your brother for Yank military and phoned here looking for me. That was right after they called the police."

"There were reports made? Photographs taken?"

"You don't want to see the pictures, ma'am."

Rae Connolly nodded decisively. "Yes, I do."

Jeff nodded, opened his private safe and handed her a file folder.

Like I said, she was tough. She stared at each of the three photos of her baby brother and his shoe for a minute or so.

Few of us are tough enough to look death in the face that long without effect. Major Connolly suddenly got to her feet. "Where's your toilet, Captain Masters? I need to call a time-out here."

The Uaddan manager, bartender and pool boy were helpful and cooperative. Jeff was a customer as well as a cop. When he vouched for Rae as the sister of the man they'd found dead, the three of them bowed and kissed her hands. Each told his story, but only the bartender's account was important. Far from drinking heavily and alone at the bar, he said, Ron had nursed one beer, stayed about an hour and lost perhaps ten dollars at craps before disappearing down the long hall that led to the locker rooms, pool deck and parking lot. He was found the next morning by the pool boy. The manager telephoned the authorities and then the American police. The door to the minaret stairway, usually locked and in any case hard to find, was ajar when the Tripoli police checked it after the body was taken away.

The police captain initially refused to discuss the case with a foreign woman, even the grieving sister of a possible murder victim. Jeff applied a gallon or two of charm and sweet mint tea and the man eventually cooperated, summoning the two officers who'd answered the call from the Uaddan manager. The lost shoe was mentioned, suggestive of struggle rather than suicide. The minaret balcony had a parapet wall that would be difficult, though perhaps not impossible, to trip and fall over. The officer who'd spotted the shoe suggested that such an accident would be somewhat more likely if the person was drunk, stoned or blind. The chief himself added that his own clerk had checked record books as far back as they went. No one else had ever fallen, jumped or been thrown from the Uaddan minaret's balcony. And, of course, no, they had no suspect in hand or in mind. No one admitted seeing anything more than what the Uaddan bartender had related to Rae. No snitches had come forward, seeking rewards for information. No further clues had turned up.

Rae had known none of these details.

At the O club, Rae and I spoke to the manager, both regular bartenders and a waiter. Same story. Ron limited himself to the two-for-one beer special and a bowl of chips at weekly happy hours. If he dined with Jeff or a table of junior officers he might take one beer or glass of wine. As far as the staffers could remember, the lieutenant had never been seen drunk or even unsteady on his feet. And at this O club, as I explained to his sister, such abstemious behavior was virtually unique.

Everything fit the picture I already had: Ron Connolly was sober, conservative, unlikely to take big risks and scared to death. He'd ignored the agreement to consult Jeff or me if handed another set of secret orders. He'd played the patsy one time too many and paid the ultimate price.

Jeff and I had to work the next morning. Rae, who was staying at a budget hotel in town, slept off her jet lag. Thinking she might enjoy something local but safe, the three of us met for lunch at the BX snack bar, the only place on base that served couscous, the Libyan national dish. Jeff told the counterman he'd have the camel couscous with hot sauce, and winked. Rae didn't catch the joke. Marines don't overvalue irony or a sense of humor. "Make it two," she said automatically. I said I'd have a grilled cheese sandwich and French fries.

Jeff found a table at the far end of the room, away from the crowd, and we got down to business. "Your brother took emergency leave in November," he said. "We don't know where he went or what he did. The emergency number he left was disconnected. Do you know where he was?"

Rae put down the bottle of Pepsi she'd been sipping. "As a matter of fact, yes, I do."

"Your brother was worried about something and wanted to fix it. That's how I see this."

"Well, you saw him every day, Captain Masters. What do you think he was worried about?"

"What I think, Major, is that it didn't get fixed."

"He visited me, Captain. In Washington. We discussed the situation. He was already in pretty deep. Mixed up with operations he had no reason to know about. I thought I could stop it or, at least, protect him in some way. I told him to get back to Wheelus, sit tight and do nothing. I ran out of time."

A boy delivered two plates of couscous topped with chicken stew and wedges of local flat bread and a plastic basket containing the sandwich, fries and a packet of ketchup. Jeff and I exchanged looks.

"We told him the same thing," I said. "And near as we can figure, he paid no attention."

"He promised to find one of us if he got hit up on again," Jeff said. "But maybe he had no choice. Looks that way to me."

"Let's stop dancing around this, gentlemen. Do you know what I do at the Pentagon?"

I hadn't even known she worked at the Pentagon. But it was logical, since Elmo McAddams had alerted us that she was on the way. "No, ma'am. What?"

"Marine intelligence. My brother was being used by people he didn't know. He hoped and prayed I could find out what—who—was behind it. I thought I could, too."

Jeff dug into his lunch. "We're on the same page, ma'am."

"This isn't really camel, is it?"

"No, ma'am, it's chicken. You have to go downtown to get real camel. Your hotel probably serves it. Won't be on the menu in English, though."

"My brother suspected that Air Force personnel were illegally trafficking in arms, maybe to splinter groups in the Middle East. He was sure they'd set him up as the fall guy in case the business became known. He said somebody close to the wing commander checked it out for him but swore it was an off-the-books operation that didn't concern Wheelus. Wheelus was just a transit point for off-shore NATO operations." She'd stopped eating. "Mediterranean operations. That was you, Captain Harding?"

"That was the story given to me, ma'am. I didn't swear it was true. No way I could vouch for it."

"By who?"

"I'm the commander's aide, ma'am. You understand my position? I've said more than I ought to already."

Jeff set down his fork and wiped his mouth. "They flew in here, handed him one-page sets of orders, told him he couldn't mention any of it, made him transport various things into town, then grabbed the orders back and flew back out."

"Yes, that's essentially what he told me."

"My air cops shook down his truck one day and informed me about the probable contraband, cases of G.I. rations, God knows what else. Ordinance, we believe. Mortars and shells."

Where does General McAddams figure in this?

"So you went where, ma'am? Air Force intelligence? NIS? OSI?"

The look she threw me would have burned the skin off a boot Marine. "Captain, I'm a mid-level information manager, not the commanding general. I contacted an Air Force officer at the Pentagon. His wife and my ex-husband went to school together."

"General McAddams?"

Flame-thrower look number two.

"You are indeed well informed, Captain Harding. Are we playing games? I didn't cross the Atlantic to be toyed with."

"A buddy of mine, another officer here, he used to fly with the general. They keep in contact. He tipped us off somebody was coming. Didn't say who. That's all."

You're talking too much, Joe. Cool your jets.

"General McAddams promised to see what he could find out. He got back to me last week. He also cited NATO but said the operation had been shut down."

I traded her one for one. "I was told it had been shut down before your brother——before what happened. That was way before Christmas."

"Looks like it hadn't been." Jeff wiped his empty plate with half a slice of bread. "I mean if we assume the same outfit made a Santa Claus run in here and leaned on your brother again, something must of got fouled up and they terminated him."

Rae drew a breath and crossed herself.

Jeff finished his bread. "We need more information."

Actually, we had plenty more but Jeff and I were playing our cards close to our chests. Rae Connolly wasn't making it easy to like her, or to cooperate. But then she held a somewhat different hand. I figured we'd put it all together eventually and, bingo, we'd nail her brother's killers and get medals.

I told them I had to take care of something at the office, something I'd forgotten. Walking back to headquarters, I ran through the whole scene again. Something didn't feel right. It seemed odd that Elmo McAddams had given her essentially the same story Colonel Swanson had given Ops to pass on to me. From the intelligence the three of us had traded over lunch, it seemed likely that it had been a dodge when

Ops repeated it the previous fall and a dodge when the major talked to McAddams. It seemed likely that the operation hadn't been shut down even now. They might just be looking for another patsy.

Do I have to quit trusting Ops? He wouldn't betray me and Jeff. Would he? We're his buddies. Would he lie and mislead us if ordered to? OK, OK, it's not impossible, is it?.

Knowingly or not, he'd fed us a line that appeared to be false. We'd now have to check everything twice.

I asked Airman Wilson to pay another visit to air traffic control to recheck flight ops records. I wanted to know if a C-130 had flown in shortly before Lieutenant Connolly's death. What about the plane carrying the bag-and-body team? From where, to where? We needed more information.

He briefed me the next morning. The flight that arrived on the day Connolly's body was found was a routine, round-trip service between Southeast Asia, the Mideast and CONUS—the continental United States—operating every ten days to two weeks. Flight records were incomplete. The service stopped at Wheelus for refueling only sporadically, more often at Torrejon, Naples or Rhine-Main. Tail numbers were not always supplied nor were the aircraft commanders' names and rank always given.

A coincidence or murder according to schedule?

Further, during the ten days prior to Connolly's death, no planes fitting the description of either the bag-and-body plane or the Dover-Korat service arrived at Wheelus. Traffic always slows down around the holidays.

Maybe his death has nothing to do with the off-books deliveries. And yet Elmo McAddams's remarks to Rae suggest that it does. How many other guys are reading from the same script?

Not only did we not have the whole story, in other words. From what we knew so far, the weapons and Ron's death had to be in some way connected.

Later that day, Colonel Swanson asked me what information we'd turned up. I answered truthfully, without details, not much.

We took Rae to the Swan restaurant that night, again choosing seats away from other people. On the way into town, with Jeff driving for once, Rae asked, as if casually, "You are aware that the Company has some kind of operation in Tripoli?"

"The Company?" That was not news. For all I knew, the CIA ran spies in every capital city in the world. But I was still playing it safe. I hesitated. "Ma'am?"

What did surprise me was that she added, "The Company lost a man who was based here last year. Do you suppose it could all be related? I should probably look into that, back at the office."

She worked in intelligence. She was some kind of spy. So it made sense that she thought like a spy. And had resources we could never match.

Pete Ferrette, the CIA station chief, had supposedly died when the C-130 skidded off the runway. Had he been replaced? Were under-cover operations proceeding normally in Libya? I could hardly ask the ambassador. And if I looked into such a matter on my own, without a plausible need to know, I'd be taking needless risks.

Rae's suggested line of inquiry made sense.

But Jeff didn't want to connect the dots, even in the privacy of the Pontiac. "You know, ma'am, any weapons shipments or black transactions would presumably be cleared by State, the Department of the Air Force or some other agency. They'd be highly classified. Any loose-cannon cowboys peddling weapons on the open market would get nailed. The materials are numbered and have to be accounted for."

Except when they don't.

I could think of numerous examples of expensive equipment going missing at Wheelus and later being written off as expendable.

"Ma'am," Jeff continued, "You ought to think twice before mentioning this matter to anyone else. Could get dangerous for you."

"It's about my baby brother, Captain."

"No, ma'am," I said. "With all due respect, it may not be. Not most of it."

I didn't mention the copies and carbon flimsies stashed in my office safe. I didn't mention that one of the men on the wrecked plane cursed when he recognized her brother, and disappeared the next day. Those were valuable cards. I'd play them if and when necessary.

Jeff was right about danger, though. He, his Sergeant Ward and half a dozen air cops knew about the weapons and purloined G.I. rations. None of that could really be considered a secret.

Dinner wasn't much fun. I drank too much red wine. We got no further work done. With Jeff again driving, we dropped Rae at her hotel and headed for the base. About halfway there, Jeff burped, rubbed his gut and said, "She's a real ball buster."

"I thought you liked ball-busting women."

"Not her kind. Wouldn't surprise me if she's trained to kill with her bare hands."

"You want to turn around and go visit Signora Agrigento?"

"Get off my ass, Joe. I've got to give that up. Like Ops said."

"Did you get a new *Playboy* in the mail?"

"I'm hoping they'll give me a female officer for a toilet mate. Say, a good looking young nurse, just asking to be broken in."

"Dream on, Casanova."

"Who?"

After Rae Connolly left Libya, we discovered that she'd been running investigations all over town. She contacted Hal Denman and Colonel Opstein without telling us. She interviewed troopers in the motor pool, an ambulance driver from base hospital and most of the Uaddan casino staff, all without our knowledge or permission. She left messages for Tech Sergeant Ward, but he referred her back to Jeff.

Ball-busters are bad news but usually manageable. Rae Connolly was another ticking time bomb. If she tossed my name and Jeff's into the spy-world hopper back in the States, and the off-the-books guys looked us up, we might wish we'd merely been grabbed, drugged and thrown off a minaret.

Jeff had drawn a new toilet mate, the replacement motor pool officer, a nervous, overweight Mormon from Utah. I was damned if I'd have him as a workout buddy. As far as I was concerned, if his sacred underpants caught on fire, somebody else would have to hose him down.

CHAPTER 7

DOMESTIC RELATIONS

"Get out of my personal business, Captain."

Jeff was devastated and I didn't know why.

"It ain't your affair. Leave me the fuck alone."

We'd been jogging around the track. Ten or fifteen minutes in, when we'd just broken a sweat, I'd said, "So where'd you go?"

Jeff's pace didn't slow for another dozen yards. But the tears started down his hard, tanned face as soon as I spoke. His voice was a wrenching sob when he muttered, "I'm just fucked, that's all."

He'd disappeared from Wheelus without a word almost a week earlier. When I stopped by the AP station to check on him, his office door was closed. Sergeant Ward said he'd requested emergency leave. He was gone six days.

Why didn't he say anything to me? Maybe we could have talked through it. At least he might have been better prepared for whatever crisis he had to face.

Now he was lying on the packed sand at the edge of the track, arms around his chest, barely holding himself together, weeping like a boy whose dog has been hit by a speeding car. He was wearing tan workout shorts and his favorite T-shirt, special-ordered by his mom back in Arkansas. The Air Force Commendation ribbon was splashed across the front, the Vietnam Service ribbon covered his back.

I dropped down beside him, kneeling, patting his shoulder, rubbing his thick, muscular neck. "Get it all out, Jeff. Nobody's around. Cry. Shout. Fuck the world. It's OK. I'm here."

"Get your hands off me. You can't help. I'm fucked."

"The OSI's not after you again, are they? What?"

Still sobbing, Jeff rolled away, escaping what I'd intended as buddy-to-buddy consolation. Surely he hadn't misinterpreted my gentle manhandling as overly familiar contact? He knew me better than that.

Still facing away, he sobbed for a couple more minutes, racked by hacking, heaving cries toward the end, before beginning to simmer down.

Finally, pushing himself up into a sitting position he swabbed his face with the oversize Commendation ribbon.

"Let's go get a shower," I said.

"Nobody's seeing me like this, Joe. Nobody else."

"OK, let's just sit here."

"Yeah, let's sit here."

"Only tell me what's going on."

"You wouldn't understand."

"Jeff, I took care of you when you got hurt bad. You took care of me when I was sick. You drove me to the hospital when I got burned. Try me. Trust me."

And so it all came out. Toward the end of February, he'd received another letter from his wife. She was still unwilling to come to Libya, much less live in an off-base villa. This time, she'd added that the marriage had probably been a mistake in the first place. Played against Rae Connolly's family-centered hunt for information, plus Jeff's growing guilt at buying punishment from whores, he'd decided he must act to save his marriage. After a quick, private talk with Colonel Opstein, he flew home to try to persuade his wife to change her mind.

He found her in maternity clothes. He'd been back to Little Rock once, halfway through his eighteen-month unaccompanied tour, but at that time she'd claimed to be on the rag. It had been ten months since they'd had real sexual intercourse. Doing the math was too easy, too ugly, too fast. He'd lost faith in his church—or at least in the lying, deceitful Chaplain Jenner—months ago. Now his wife had lost faith in him.

"I didn't even stop and say hello to my mom, Joe. I didn't even unpack. I just called another taxi and hauled ass back to the airport."

Jeff was my closest straight friend. He knew more about me and my personal business than even Uncle Carl. He'd been good enough to look the other way when

I screwed up big time. Now he needed help. This was a disaster for a young, married officer, especially if he decided to make the Air Force his career. And he was right. I had no idea what to do except listen, or how to fix whatever could still be fixed.

So I suggested the standard military solution to any really big problem: Drink the club's bar dry.

Of course that didn't fix anything. After a six-course supper of Jack Daniel's and water, we were on our way back to the BOQ when Jeff started crying again.

"The bitch. I love her, how could she do this? She wasn't even going to tell me, just give him up for adoption. I'm fucked, Joe."

"We've got to talk to Ops. He'll know what to do."

"No, no. I can't face him like this. I'm fucked, Joe. I'm fucked."

I waited three or four days, noticed that Jeff was hitting the club bar hard every night, gave Ops a call and respectfully suggested that he invite Jeff to join him in a power-lift workout followed by a man-to-man talk. Jeff ended up crying on Ops's shoulder the way he more-or-less had on mine. But Ops couldn't fix it, either.

Bastard children, lonely husbands buying off-base relief, wayward wives in serious trouble—those were problems few gay servicemen had to face. We created temporary, and occasionally even long-term, partnerships disguised as buddy-ships. As long we did our jobs well, nobody in the Air Force noticed or cared. The wise and well-adjusted among us made the most of time spent together. If difficulties arose, or assignments separated us for too long to bear, we split. Emotionally, we traveled light. We had to.

"Even if you divorce her you'll have to have to pay child support," I told Jeff a couple of nights later. We were sweating out kinks in the steam room after our workouts. Nobody else was around. For once I had a towel modestly draped across my lap. Jeff's was wound tight around his waist.

"He's not mine. She. It."

"I don't think it matters. You're married to the mother so it's presumed to be yours. Legally. I think."

"You don't know shit. You're a—probably not going to get married."

We both knew the term he almost used.

"My parents divorced when I was a kid. My father drank and didn't pay child support a lot of times. My mother got the sheriff after him."

"You were legal. Leave it alone. I'll figure something out."

A couple of days later, during Colonel Swanson's staff meeting, it hit me, or rather an idea did. The judge advocate, or base lawyer, a captain named Sarah Louise Harper, was seated across the table. The glazed expression on her face implied she had better things to do. I decided to supply one. I knew how to work the system

After the meeting, I took her aside and asked a hypothetical question, describing Jeff's dilemma but assigning the case to an unnamed NCO. Captain Harper replied that she would contact her counterpart at the base nearest to where the wife resided, and they'd go from there, but that she'd have to interview the serviceman first.

Although Jeff wasn't happy at what I'd done, he listened.

"Think of it like this," I said. "You got your jollies with Mistress Renata and a few times with Signora Agrigento's girl. Mrs. Jeff made mistakes, too. So you're even, in a way."

"I'm a man. I've got needs. I'm a stupid cop but I've got needs."

"Don't be stupid on this one. Say she gets a divorce next week and asks for child support and alimony. She'd win, you'd lose—including half your paycheck every other week and probably one of your nuts."

"Why don't you stay out of this? I'll think of something."

"You're fucked, you said so yourself. Somebody's got to take care of you. What are buddies for?"

"I don't trust lawyers, Joe."

"Trust *me*, Jeff. Trust *me*. Do you want me to go with you to see Captain Harper?"

"Like I want a case of crabs. It'll be bad enough going alone."

Airman Dottie Bacon held up a framed black-and-white photograph, one of several such grip-and-grin shots scattered around the wing commander's private office. "Who's this with the Colonel?"

A much younger, rawboned Swanson in a cadet's dress uniform was shaking hands—and staring in utter admiration—at a buzzard-faced old man wearing a tweed suit.

"Douglas MacArthur," I answered. "He was a top general in World War Two and Korea. He thought he was going to be president."

"Handsome guy," Dottie purred.

I wondered if Dottie had ever heard of MacArthur. Or the Korean war.

Airman Wilson was tidying stacks of briefing books and papers on the colonel's desk. "He's a little old for you, Peaches. Anyway, he's dead."

"I mean the colonel, silly."

Mentally stripping off Cadet Swanson's frogged jacket, striped pants and wheel cap, I decided he'd definitely have earned a second look in my college locker room, maybe even an invitation to a slow, sweaty wrestling match in a deserted, darkened gym. I wondered if "Duty Honor Country" was tattooed on the West Point graduate's arm. Just as quickly, I decided I had no need, much less the desire, to know.

Wilson hooted. "You're aiming high, girl. You figure you'll catch his attention with those grapefruits you been shoplifting in your Maidenform?"

"I've seen your chicken chest and jelly belly on the beach, Buster. What I figure is that the biggest fruit in San Francisco wouldn't give you a tumble."

Wilson glanced at me, concluded I was neutral in this game, and gave as good as he got. "Word in my barracks, girl, is that you're basically the salad bar at the NCO club."

"Yeah? Well, from what I hear, nobody in your slack-ass barracks will drop a cake of soap when you're within ten yards of the showers."

I had to break up this undisciplined exchange or break out laughing. "OK, troops. I'd like to remind you that military courtesy, mutual respect and teamwork are keys to an effective organization *and* outstanding performance reports. Before you take off for supper, I want both of you to type me up a five-point list of specific suggestions for improving the overall efficiency of this office. A full page at least."

They scowled at each other, trading blame.

"Both of you," I added, "could benefit from more attention to proper dress and deportment."

If I sounded a bit too prim and proper, a confirmed bachelor of the old school, it didn't matter. I couldn't risk having either of them mouthing off in front of the colonel, another officer or a senior NCO. It was then ten minutes till quitting time. Missing early chow might make an impression. The last thing I needed in my office was more jokes about drop-the-soap games and San Francisco fairies.

Hal Denman didn't have "Duty Honor Country" or anything else tattooed on his compact, muscular body—and he looked fine. By nine that night I'd seen most of it—he was still wearing white athletic socks and Hanes briefs. As usual I liked what I saw. When he reached over and stroked my face, one of those big fat romantic clichés hit me hard: my heart skipped a beat. I grinned. He grinned.

Having this strong, physically magnificent older man as a beat-off buddy was a turn-on, a comfort, the kind of lesson in mutual respect I couldn't share with my

misbehaving clerks—or anyone else. Sure, there were occasional misunderstand-
ings. Neither of us was the shy, retiring type. There were also joyous surprises.
We were friends as well as each other's safety valves. From what I'd read about it
in classics and ancient history classes, soldiers like us have shared our bodies and
protected each other from exposure, embarrassment and danger ever since war was
invented.

We were stretched out on the hand-made Oriental rug in his living room. We'd
started on the leather couch, fully clothed, talking. Hal laughed at my account of
clerks trading insults but backed me completely in the matter of discouraging off-
color, suggestive banter in the office.

"Won't do," he said. "Got to keep it clean. Don't let the boys insult the females, you know? Separate 'em. Like in school."

If Hal considered himself gay, queer, a deviant homosexual or anything less
than a regular guy, he never said so to me. His first boxing coach had given his
boys back rubs and warm oil rubdowns after their fights, and that was the defining
chapter in Hal's sexual education. Like me, he'd traded favors in bath houses. He'd
hired masseurs who didn't mind a little extra work for a bigger tip. He was aware
that an open door at a residential YMCA or visiting officers' quarters was a signal
with only one meaning. As far as I knew, he'd never been with a woman. He'd never exactly said that, though, and I didn't ask. And then he met Lieutenant Colonel
Elmo McAddams, pilot to his navigator, and decided he'd found what he wanted.
So he stopped fooling around for a long while. But McAddams was married and
ambitious. Moving up the Air Force ladder, the flyer-turned-administrator was also
able to take care of his boy, ship Hal from safe base to safe base—and keep him out
of Vietnam. Wheelus was the latest stop. Then Hal seduced me, it all felt right, and
I was happy to follow his lead and do what he wanted sexually.

I touched the front of his stiffly tented briefs. He shivered and closed his dark
eyes.

I gave the tent pole a squeeze. "You could do some real damage with this con-
cealed weapon. Let me get these off you, OK, Rocky?"

He let me. "I'm not big like you, Joe. I measured. Back in college. I'm kind of
average. Yeah, do that. Yeah, yeah. Oh, fuck, yeah."

"You're about as average as a Cadillac Eldorado. Roll over. Let me rub your
back first. We'll get to the stick shift in a minute"

It was months before Hal grew entirely comfortable letting me get him off.
Unlike his old coach, too many men he'd been with took a lot more than they gave,
leaving him to finish himself.

He rolled over and I straddled him, kneading his back and shoulders and thick upper arms. I was wearing only a T-shirt and by this point in the session I'd usually have been poking his butt with a hard cock. Not that I'd try to enter him; we'd discussed that and he'd said no dice. My pokes were just sex play, guy-guy roughhousing, exciting myself, getting aroused and ready for my own rubdown's countdown.

This time, it wasn't happening. My penis was as limp as wet Kleenex. I groped myself. Nothing. I looked down at Hal's massive shoulders, his shapely neck, his trim ears and saw the thin wiry frame of my schoolboy tennis partner. I humped Hal's butt. It was Cotton Boardman beneath me in a Swiss hotel bed, and I was hurting him.

Hal began to thrash beneath me. "Lemme, lemme, I gotta, Joe, fuck, yeah. Oh, God, Joe."

I let him roll over beneath me, handled his erect tits, tried to French kiss him. He forced my hands lower, positioned them around his leaking rod and began fucking the double fist. As we'd often done before, we quickly fell into a mutual pistoning push-push that didn't last long. "Don't stop, don't stop, Joe. That's so good. Jesus. No, oh no, that's my fucking knockout, I'm down for the count. God, Joe. God, Joe. Oh God. Fuck. Fuckin'-A, Joe. Fuckin'-A"

Sometimes he went first, sometimes I did. We rarely came off together, and then only if one of us was much hornier than the other.

We took a five-minute break before Hal started on me. The backrub felt great, my neck and ears were kissed, my butt deeply, greasily fingered, and for a few minutes, I started getting aroused, leaking, lengthening out.

I rolled over and looked up. It wasn't Cotton astride me, pinching my tits, stroking my balls and face, kissing my neck, playing with my ass, it was Hal. I closed my eyes and tried to turn Hal's hands into Cotton's. Cotton was there for a moment or two, above me, and then he wasn't. I pictured other men who'd turned my sexuality inside out—Duane, Kim, Thomas Philips back at Vanderbilt.

Nothing. I wanted Cotton and he wasn't here. Pushing Hal's big, straining hands away, I tried to do the job myself. Again nothing. Ice cold nothing.

Now I just wanted to just get it over with, ride the horse home. And I'd turned into a frustrated, emasculated mule.

"Never mind," I finally said. "I can't tonight. It's OK, Rocky."

Hal slipped down beside me, draped his heavy right arm across my still-heaving chest and whispered, "Sure, it's OK, Joe. Happens. I understand."

Of course he didn't understand. He knew next to nothing about my friendship with Cotton and I couldn't explain what was wrong. Jeff's desperate words as he lay sobbing on the running track crossed my mind. *"I'm fucked. I'm just fucked, that's all."*

I wanted to spend the whole night in Hal's strong, protective arms but I couldn't even do that. I'd stayed over a couple of times but it wasn't safe. Being seen leaving another man's room early in the morning was a risk seldom worth taking.

I was fucked. And if Cotton's father succeeded in convincing his mother that I'd compromised him, I was double fucked, triple, quadruple, name your price.

Another brandy didn't help. I put on my clothes, returned to my room, fell into bed and slept no more than a couple of hours.

So I wasn't at my best the next morning when I opened the door to Colonel Swanson's office and found him with his pants and boxers around his ankles. His back was to me, his blouse was pulled up and I got the whole picture in one Technicolor instant: long, strong, hairy legs; tight, pallid, hairy ass; slim hips thrusting and pounding, somebody seated in his desk chair, taking it.

He heard me, half-turned and pulled out. Like most of us tall, lanky guys, he was hung in proportion.

Airman Bacon occupied his chair. She'd missed her chance to finish him off. Without ever quite looking at me, the colonel turned away, calmly pulled up his pants, stuffed his blouse and hard cock down where they belonged, buttoned his buttons, zipped his zipper and fastened his web belt. Dottie meanwhile tidied her uniform and stalked out of the office, snatching up her steno pad as she went.

The colonel then seated himself where Dottie had been, cool as banana ice cream. "Yes? What's up, Joe?" It was almost as if nothing out of the ordinary had happened. And, in a way, that was true enough. He was the boss and, if he acted as though nothing had happened, officially nothing had. Up to a point, full colonels and generals could create their own reality. We lesser mortals had to live with it.

When I thought about it later, the interrupted blow job seemed like a perfect gotcha, one more get-out-of-jail-free card. I'd caught the old man behaving in a way that was not only conduct unbecoming an officer and gentleman but sexually abusing a subordinate over whom he held the power of life and death. This violation of military discipline and good order ought to be ten times worse than my beat-off sessions with Hal. I held the colonel's career in my hand.

By that night, however, I'd faced facts. Whatever her motivation, Dottie had been willing to satisfy Swanson's needs. If called on it, she'd refuse to admit guilt or lodge a complaint. If I said anything, it might backfire. Payback could be a below-average performance evaluation from Swanson and dashed hopes of ever making even major.

Why didn't he take her back to his villa? How are we going to work together after this? I'm fucked. I got what I must have wanted—a good look at the old goat's ass and ram's-horn cock—and it could cost me. Why the hell did I have to see this? The two of them could gang up on me, my word against theirs. I'm dog meat. I am royally fucked.

By suppertime, I was tired, confused, horny and worried sick, all in all a dangerous combination. I missed Cotton and feared I'd never see him again. I couldn't get the picture of the steel-hard, half-naked colonel out of my mind. I wanted more than a hand job from Hal. I needed something far hotter than I was likely find in the steam room at the base gym. Signora Agrigento's studs for hire were out of the question.

The Uaddan casino attracted what passed for an international crowd, not to mention a fair sampling of call girls and hustlers. It wouldn't be San Francisco but I thought it might do. I showered, put on civvies, drove into town and ordered a beer at the bar. Although I was known there, it seemed a better bet, and no less safe, than my other options.

The long bar was busy but not crowded. I chose the middle seat among five empty stools at the darker end of the room. Fifteen minutes later a burly, crew-cut guy, obviously American and perhaps five years my senior, put his hand on the stool to my right.

"This seat taken?"

He was wearing a heavily carved wedding ring, Hawaiian aloha shirt, chinos, rawhide work boots and Jade East cologne.

"Make yourself at home, sir." This looked promising.

He stuck out his hand. "Call me Jay."

I told him my name was Duane. He ordered a double Martini, up. I said I usually drank brandy or Jack in the Black but was watching it tonight.

"How come, pal?"

"I didn't get much sleep last night. Hard day at work. I'm kind of on edge."

Hard day. That's cute, Joe.

He got the message. "There's things you can do about that."

"I've sort of run out of ideas."

"That so? Hmm, well. See those girls down the bar, them two hookers? One of them'll take your edge off."

"I'm not really into that." Which was certainly true.

"That so?" He sipped his drink and neither one of us said anything for a while. Then his left knee touched my right, just for a moment.

This may work out.

My right knee, as if it had a mind of its own, moved toward his left. Chino-to-chino, neither of us broke the contact for fifteen or twenty seconds. Then he turned to me, scowled manfully and placed his big open hand on my inner thigh, halfway between my knee and my crotch. "I'm not that way, pal. So watch it."

He had ice-water eyes, blue and clear. His hand stayed where it was. His signals were definitely mixed. I figured he was more than a little drunk.

"That was your knee touching mine, buddy."

He squeezed my leg and shifted on his stool so that he had me between his knees.

I touched the knee that was hidden under the bar. The room was fairly dark anyway and a glance around told me nobody was watching us. "You're a big guy, Jay. I never saw you here before."

He put his hand on mine, lightly rubbing my knuckles with his fingertips. "You, too, Duane, a big guy. I don't get into town that much."

He drained his drink. The bartender set down another, as if automatically.

"It's good you're here tonight."

"Yeah, I got lucky."

You sure did.

"Won a couple hundred shooting craps." His voice sounded only moderately happy about winning a bundle. He had scars on his face and hands, a roughneck's scars. His mouth was a thin line, his hair cropped as short as mine.

You're on a roll, Jay.

"When I come into town, I always get me a good room upstairs, one that looks out on the water. Treat myself. Company's paying, see. Put it on the old expense account."

I was too aroused and sex-hungry to even think of the fake minaret.

"Has a good view, huh?"

"You want to see it?" He groped me lightly. "I got a bottle up there." Withdrawing his hand, he finished his drink.

"Yeah, Jay. OK, sure. Let's go upstairs and see the view." My balls had already started to sizzle.

Once upstairs, the only view I wanted was the sight of Jay with his clothes off. That ultimately proved shadowy but distinct enough; the bathroom light stayed on.

Even in partial darkness, it was clear that the man was built like a hockey player: big arms, thick thighs and wide shoulders. His face, neck and lower arms were tan; the rest of him was pale as Colonel Swanson's butt and mostly hairless. He had a tattoo on his right biceps, presumably a woman's name, "Dorris," encircled in a bleeding heart. There was an ID bracelet on his right wrist and a waterproof Rolex on his left. Like Swanson, he was almost as tall as I am. His hard cock was at least as long as mine, thicker and already leaking like a busted fire hydrant.

I'd gotten my shoes and shirt off, and was unzipping my chinos, when he pushed me roughly down on the double bed. "Wastin' time, pal," he said, slurring slightly. "I'll do that."

My chinos and briefs were on the floor in one swift motion and he was on top of me, growling deep in his throat, pinching my tits, snuffling my armpits, scuffing my balls and inner thighs with his buzzed scalp and whiskered chin, shoving his cock between my legs and riding me like a pony. I was never in control and, for the next couple of hours, didn't want to be. No strong, angry alpha had ever dominated me like this. Instinctively, I realized he was going to give me what I needed no matter what I did, and that I probably couldn't stop him anyway, not until he'd satisfied himself.

This was no rubdown, no kid stuff. At one point, for instance, I kissed, sucked and then bit down on one of his nipples. He slapped me. "Watch those teeth, pal." I didn't mind at all; liked it, in fact. And when he immediately followed the slap with deep kisses, I arched my back under him and wrapped my legs around his hips, as submissive as I'd ever been in my life.

One of his thick fingers, then two, finally three teased into my asshole, probing, stretching, sending shock waves from my prostate to my balls and dick head. Slowly removing his fingers after what seemed much too short a time, he filled the empty space with something rigid and rubbery, greased, almost cold, like dead flesh. I groaned.

I'm Cotton, I suddenly thought. *And Jay's me, and maybe I'm learning something from this, learning, fucking learning, fucking—he's teaching me, ah, God, yes.*

Removing the dildo, he rubbed it up and down my dangerously hard dick. I almost came.

"No question," Jay muttered, licking the dildo before tossing it away. "Anybody could tell you're in need of a good fucking. "You want it, pal?"

I nodded. He filled the empty space again, this time with himself. As he started to pump into me, he shook his head, dropped his jaw and stared into my eyes. The look on his face was that of a stallion on a mare, instinctive and animalistic. When he came closer to his first climax, his expression changed to something between disgusted and dutiful, as if he might change his mind. He didn't.

He never hurt or degraded me. He simply forced me to accept new limits, to beg for more of something I'd never known existed, to taste my own juice mixed with his and wish I could shoot as much semen for him as a horse could piss. He licked me in places that had never been licked, made me shudder and lose track of who was doing what to who, turned me into a groaning caricature of Hal Denman at his outermost edge, "Fuckin'-A, pal. Fuckin'-A, pal, yeah, fuckin'-A."

Jay brought me off twice, once with his mouth, then with his hand as he fucked me a second time. In some ways, until I met this domineering man, I'd been as innocent as a weanling colt. I'd never experienced anything remotely like it, or him. Whatever the wedding ring stood for, it sure didn't mean he went only with women.

Eventually, we separated and fell asleep, our backs to each other on the soggy, stinking double bed, me with the top sheet pulled up, him a foot away, naked.

Somewhere before dawn, turning over in his sleep, his left arm landed heavily on my side. A loving embrace it wasn't. He began thrashing, mumbling, crying out, grabbing at my side, and was suddenly possessed by a vicious dream. I tried to touch him, comfort him, lure him back from hell. He grabbed my arms, pushed me away, tossed his head from side to side, began crying out, "Not Cheeto, not Bird, what about the Zulu? No, God, no. Not the Zulu," repeating these names three or four times, in any order, until the dream, or at least the outward signs of it, disappeared and he fell silent.

We slept again. When I awoke a second time, his arms were around me, holding me tight, as a drowning man might hold onto a life ring thrown from a ship.

"You had a dream," I whispered. "A nightmare."

He answered without opening his eyes. "My unit got taken out. I was on leave. Still am. Maybe a day or two AWOL for all I know. Have to check."

Military. It figures.

"That's tough, Jay. Tet was it? Two men I knew bought it up by the DMZ."

"One man standing." His voice was groggy, his breath an ugly combination of gin, cigar smoke and what the two of us had done hours earlier. "Bangkok fuckin' airport, there I was. Phoned in. Nobody to report to. Me, I'm it. No site. No unit. Nothing."

This man is fucked worse than you are, Joe. Be gentle.

"You'll get through it. The service takes care of its own. Cheeto, Zulu and who was it? The Bird? They didn't die for nothing. The war's not over yet."

"The fuck?" His hands moved up to my shoulders, way too close to my neck. "Wha'd you say?"

"Those names. You were saying them in your sleep, calling to them, something like that. Saying 'No, no.'"

Suddenly he sat up, rolled away, hoisted his legs over his side of the bed and hunched forward, looking at the floor. "It's a movie, pal."

Maybe he's still drunk.

"Yeah, pal. Now I remember. I had that dream before. It's an old war flick I saw when I was a kid. Aldo Rae and Montgomery Clift, can't remember the other guy. Cheeto, Bird and the Zulu are soldiers. They get tortured and killed by the ChiComs. Only the commander, the Old Lion, escapes. John Wayne, the Duke, he played the Old Lion."

I'd never heard of the movie but that didn't mean anything. Jay was older and not every B movie played in Ocala or Nashville.

Jay hauled himself to his feet, said he had to get moving, had to catch his flight out to the oil field and needed a quick shower. He didn't even glance at me again.

Clearly he wasn't planning to buy me breakfast. I knew a brush-off when I heard one. I was yesterday's fuck. Dressing fast, I left without saying goodbye.

Before leaving, I paused at the window. The view of the Mediterranean was indeed grand: ships riding at anchor in the harbor, gentle waves rolling shoreward, cars and donkey carts passing beneath me on the Mellaha corniche, graceful date-palm fronds waving like wings in the breeze.

Driving back to Wheelus, showering in the BOQ, walking to the office, I played and replayed the encounter in my mind. Was Jay the oilfield roughneck he claimed to be? Or a soldier on leave who'd just lost his unit and was mourning his buddies? Or something else? Was he really about to catch a flight or was he wild with grief and bedding anything he could get his hands on? His physical solidity, ice-water eyes, scars, tattoo, demanding tongue and high-powered energy had hit me hard. I'd never been with a man that rough. He hadn't insulted or corrupted me; the reverse was true: he'd upped my emotional and sexual ante. What had once seemed like passion was now a vanilla milkshake.

In one sense, I regretted the night and feared the consequences. People talk. I'd been picked up by a married stranger in a bar where I was known. I'd followed him upstairs.

But the night's unsentimental education also tipped the balance to the other side. Now I had to wonder if all that Vanderbilt polish and all those beat-off and suckee-fuckee sessions with Hal Denman and Duane Haynes were nothing but poor substitutes for what I suddenly believed to be the real thing. Maybe I needed a crude, dominant man and not a willing, lovesick boy like Cotton. Maybe I'd been fooling myself.

With all that on my mind I entered the office five minutes late and greeted the colonel and my clerks as if nothing at all unusual had happened the previous day.

I figured my emotional and professional lives couldn't get much more complicated or messier.

CHAPTER 8

REPORTING FOR DUTY

While I was being tutored at the Uaddan, six mortar shells landed on the British Army's tent city at Idris Airport, killing two soldiers and wounding five. A bomb squad was flown in to investigate. Conclusion: the 81 millimeter shells were British. The detachment commander was outraged; he could account for every weapon and shell in his arsenal. They hadn't been filched from him.

It took me more than a week to piece the story together. Wheelus was not officially involved so I had no need to know what happened. Before I shared my suspicions with anybody, I had to move quietly and carefully.

The first account of the attack came at an embassy briefing I attended with Colonel Swanson a few days later. The detachment commander was also present but, after beginning a brief summary of the incident, was ordered by his ambassador to be silent. When Elizabeth Boardman asked for details, her British counterpart replied that the Foreign Office "would be honoured to entertain enquiries from State."

Airman Buster Wilson, who regularly handled top secret documents, had no trouble finding an unread précis of the bomb squad's report tucked away in a new set of USAFE briefing files. No explanation for the presence of the weapons was given; no subversive or revolutionary group or person was named, no reason for the attack suggested.

At an Italian embassy reception, again accompanying Colonel Swanson but invited a second time due to my connection with the Boardmans and my friendship with Colonnello Ludovico Sforza, the military attaché, I mentioned the mortar attack to a British officer whom I knew to be part of military intelligence. The captain did a creditable job denying that his betters were in the dark about the reasons for the attack, the source of the weaponry or the identity of the attackers. He then put me in my place, suggesting that a mere colonel's aide should think twice before mentioning such matters in public. This was especially so, he concluded, to a commissioned officer of an allied power whose knowledge of such incidents he could not know—and had no reason to know.

On the surface this was a rare diplomatic gaffe. There was a chance the captain might complain to Colonel Swanson, Colonnello Sforza or Madam Ambassador. I counted it a confirmation. The mortar and shells, at least arguably, came from one of the shipments of weapons Ron Connolly had unwittingly helped to distribute.

Jeff, meanwhile, had consulted Captain Harper, the wing lawyer, and been given a set of options. A week later, having chosen the most painful and difficult course, he told her to go ahead. I took him to the Swan restaurant that night, hoping to cheer him up with minestrone, veal scaloppini and decent wine. I'd baited the invitation with news that I'd followed up on the Ron Connolly situation.

Colonel Swanson and Ambassador Boardman were seated at a table for two in the bar, deep in conversation, enjoying Florentine steaks and salads. As far as I could tell, they didn't see us.

The larger garden room wasn't crowded so Jeff and I could talk freely. He said little about his domestic problems or the meetings with Captain Harper. Instead, he told me that Agent Bivens of the OSI had called him into his office a few days earlier. Bivens opened the interview by saying he'd heard about Jeff's marital problems through channels and expressed his sympathy. He himself had had wife troubles, he'd said. They split up once but managed to patch things together.

I thought of several ugly remarks about the lack of lawyer-client confidentiality. But Jeff seemed to be a betrayal magnet: the chaplain, the whore, his wife and now the lawyer. But he didn't need me to point that out. Perhaps the regs required that Captain Harper run the matter by the OSI before taking any action. I could ask Airman Wilson to look it up.

Bivens had then turned to his real agenda: a variation on the grilling he'd once given me concerning Jeff's fitness for service and the potential risks involved when a military officer responsible for base security patronizes a free-lance whore.

"Joe, his mind's a cess pool, you know that. Dirty, filthy—"

"He's paid to think that way. You're not exactly a trusting, innocent cub scout yourself."

"Hey, I represent that remark."

"What is it you tell your air cops? Guilty until proven innocent?"

"Well, if some airman's exiting base with a tray of chow hall donuts in the back seat—"

"Or cases of canned meat and evaporated milk in a deuce-and-a-half-ton vehicle?"

"What'd you find out?"

"We'll get to that. Back to Agent Shit-for-Brains. He can be a useful bastard, you know that."

"He tried to get me to tell him Major Denman's a homo. Said he's neither married nor known to date any women. How would I know? I see him in the gym, staff meetings. He's your friend, isn't he?"

"Yes, he is."

"I'm not asking, Joe."

"He's a good man, a career officer, hard working and wishes to hell he were still flying airplanes."

"Shit, I mean everybody knows about him. He's kind of famous, Golden Gloves and all-service boxing champ, picture on the cover of *Air Force Times*. Doesn't sound like a homo to me."

Jeff was unaware of Hal's inclinations, much less that he was my beat-off buddy. I intended to keep it that way. "So what did you say?"

"Basically what you told Bivens when he tried to waste my butt—that as far as I know, Major Denman is a manly, God-fearing administrator and a former flier and prize fighter devoted to his country and married to his career. Rah, rah, rah."

"He took leave and went to Rome to see the Pope at Christmas."

"Jeez, I wish I'd known that. You think I should go back and tell him?

"Let's see if he calls me in. I can tell him."

After a break to order another bottle and finish off plates of cheese-topped soup, Jeff returned to the matter of contraband hams, weapons and his late toilet mate.

"What's cooking, Joe. You've run something down?"

"I've got an idea, a possibility of what might fit."

Jeff was more than willing to listen to my theories: Ron Connolly had been used as a go-between in the illegal trafficking of weapons. He was murdered to keep him quiet when he either started asking questions or refused to cooperate any further. His body was snatched and possibly mutilated with needles. Evidence was covered up or stolen. The weapons were not shipped out to some unknown NATO entity in the Mediterranean; they stayed in Libya and were used to attack the British.

"Who'd do all that?" Jeff finally asked. "Who could? Why?"

"You tell me. You're the security expert."

"Aside from payback over Connolly, and helping his sister, why should we get into it at all—or give a shit? This is way above our pay grades."

"Somebody doesn't like the British enough to not only kill a couple of their grunts but embarrass the Brit army publicly? They probably don't like us any better."

"Your theory says we gave 'em the weapons, right?"

"Somebody with a bunch of Air Force uniforms and a set of C-130s did."

"Doesn't make sense."

"I have a friend who says fighting the Vietnamese doesn't make sense."

"Don't say that out loud back on base. Bivens'll be on your butt like stink on shit."

"Don't you read the papers? People are marching in the streets back home. Johnson's war may bring him down."

"Hippies, quitters and peaceniks—like fuckin' Joan Baez. Gimme some more of that vino, OK? So what do we do now, us two? Why'd you tell me all this, anyway?"

"What about running my ideas past your contacts downtown? I bet the royal police aren't too happy about having their international airport used for target practice."

"And tell 'em it's the Yanks supplying the weapons?"

"No stupid-cop games, please."

"OK, OK, I'll see what I can do."

Something didn't add up. Ron Connolly had flown to Washington to ask his sister for help. Working in Marine intelligence in the Pentagon, Rae Connolly presumably had access to information about black operations and networks worldwide. She'd barely started digging when her brother was murdered. Someone she'd contacted must have tipped off the bad boys. I knew she'd consulted General Elmo McAddams only because he'd alerted us that she was on the way. But Hal Denman's mentor and longtime lover was a good guy. Who else had she talked to?

Who else knew about Ron's—and perhaps Jeff's and my—suspicions concerning contraband weapons?

And who'd tipped Bivens? He or his handlers might connect the dots—me, Hal, Jeff, Duane, Totenberg and Conroy, even Connolly or Cotton, men without women, if only temporarily—and come up with some kind of conspiracy theory. McCarthy-era homophobia wasn't that far back in the past. American politicians and preachers had employed variations on the theme since the First World War. A homosexual-feminist-Jewish-Negro-Communist conspiracy, they might claim, was intent on undermining not only the White Christian patriarchy but the war effort and the American way of life itself.

Either way, we may all be fucked. Even the straight guys like Jeff.

Three nights later, Jeff rapped on my BOQ door. "Let's go downtown. I need to." There was alcohol on his breath. Bourbon.

I thought about handing him the keys to the Pontiac but I couldn't let him go alone. Or drive my car drunk. "Cold showers and *Playboy* aren't working out for you?"

"I left word with my *policia capitano*. He's gonna get back to me."

"Thank you. We're even. Let me put on some clothes."

"Hurry it up, OK?"

Signora Agrigento let us into her parlor but dispensed with the usual greeting for Jeff and snacks for me. "You were followed here, tailed, is that right? I have to say."

Jeff had already turned toward the staircase. "How do you know?"

"I know, Captain. Maybe you should not come here again so soon." She waved to a robed presence in the shadows. "The back door. I think you go out that way now. Sabirah will guide you."

The old serving woman stepped forward, her hair and the lower half of her face swathed in a black veil. She nodded, said something we didn't understand and led us out into a stinking alley, around a corner and into the street.

Back in the car, Jeff sat hunched over, holding his knees. Along with loneliness, anger and disappointment, he'd added the crazy hornies to his list of woes. That was one problem I couldn't help him with.

Along with emotional isolation and a lengthy list of fears, I'd just added my own new problem. Was Jeff being followed or was I? Or both of us? And why?

Was this connected to Ron Connolly? Hal Denman? The old man's patronage of the brothel? What the fuck was going on?

After an early lunch four days later, I returned to headquarters and found the door to the old man's office shut.

Airman Buster Wilson, his back to me, was filing documents at the far end of the outer office. "Morning, Boss. If it *is* still morning. Hope you found something edible at the chow hall."

Airman Dottie Bacon's face was turned away. "Sir," she whispered, her voice breaking. Slowly swiveling around to greet me, she wiped her eyes with one hand and then the other. Clearly she'd been crying.

What fresh hell is this?

Fifteen minutes later, the colonel's door swung open and out sashayed a WAF airman I'd never seen before.

Airman Wilson began counting cracks in the ceiling. Airman Bacon gave the colonel the kind of look a barren old ewe might give a butcher the moment before he applied the knife to her throat. Swanson didn't return it. He soon left for lunch at the club, directing that only the most important calls be forwarded.

Late that afternoon, Airman Bacon put an incoming call through to the old man in his private office. Clearly unhappy about it, she listened for a moment, set down the receiver, rolled her eyes, muttered, "Madam Ambassador Honeycakes on the line," and stuck out her tongue.

This needed to be addressed now. "Let's go for a walk," I said. "Wilson, take over the front desk and phones, please."

"Yes, Boss. Glad to do it."

I had an idea how she must feel. The flight surgeon we'd sent to the DMZ had put his hands on me twice, not sexually but as a threat. Elizabeth Boardman had all but suggested a game of bedroom tennis. Although I'd escaped with honor each time, I'd felt trapped and threatened, my personal space invaded. The surgeon and the ambassador outranked me significantly but at least we belonged to more or less the same class. How much more humiliating must it be for a young, directionless woman to be used by a powerful older man, and then publicly tossed aside when the liaison was discovered? If she complained, he could consign her to Vietnam or North Dakota with a phone call.

"About the colonel's private life," I began.

She cut me off. "I'm so embarrassed, Captain. What you saw. I'm not that kind of girl. It was a complete mistake. I just wasn't thinking. He said we, I—"

"I don't need to know what he said, Airman."

She paid no attention. "After you, well, after you came in that time, he said we had to talk. He said we should take it easy for a while. It wasn't the first time, actually."

"He's our boss, Airman. It's not my place to judge him. The colonel is divorced, with children your age. He's an ex-jet-jockey, a risk-taker. Danger and new thrills are what they live for. A lot of unmarried fighter pilots use young, pretty young women like toilets."

She flinched. There was nothing to do but plunge on. "They like to play the field. To some of them, you're a dime a dozen, a notch in the belt. They'll say anything."

"Captain!"

"Let me finish. He put you in an impossible position. It's OK to feel embarrassed, even disappointed. Something like that happened to me—a couple of times. I know how it feels."

"You? How would—?"

"It's not the end of the world."

She sniffed. "I'll get over it. I just thought—"

"Next time, you'll know better. I can transfer you back to the commissary office if you like."

"No, no. But you and Buster—?"

"Nobody's going to talk."

"The—*he* might."

"We can't control that. Behave yourself. It'll probably blow over."

She looked away.

"So listen up," I continued. "Forget everything he told you. Forget what you hoped might happen, OK? If a woman calls him, whether she's an ambassador or an airman's wife, it's none of your business. If a woman visits him, it's none of your business. You can't react. Today you put yourself in a position where you did just that. Do you understand?"

Airman Bacon turned and showed me her tightly wrapped tits. "Captain, I still feel just awful about you seein' me in such a embarrassin' situation."

She didn't get it, or wouldn't. Had she imagined that office blow jobs counted as serious dates? She'd either learn fast or crash and burn soon enough. "Airman. I want to stay out of your personal relationships, and his. But, as your supervisor,

I'm responsible for your welfare and job performance. These were serious errors of judgment. Do you see that? In the workplace?"

She let her shoulders drop and her tits sagged. The expression on her face turned slightly accusatory. This would have been easier with the more intelligent, less mulish Buster Wilson. Man-to-man, I'd have felt slightly less embarrassed, more comfortable with the vocabulary, might even have admitted my own slight jealousy, at least to myself. But Wilson, presumably, did not suck cock, in the office or elsewhere.

"That snide remark this afternoon. What if the ambassador had heard you? You'd have been handed an Article Fifteen and busted down to airman basic."

"She didn't. I'd already put the call through."

"Don't get in the habit. Somebody else could be listening in. I repeat, the old man's calls are not your business."

"Yessir."

"Your excellent telephone etiquette is one of the reasons we brought you over here from the commissary. Don't lose that."

"Thank you, sir."

"I can see you making airman first if you pay attention to what I'm saying."

"I'll do my best, Captain."

"Good. So I'll overlook this unseemly behavior for now. But I don't want to hear or see any more sarcasm or sexing it up in my office. Do I make myself clear?"

"Yessir."

Buster Wilson was a much more appropriate and potentially appreciative target of her attentions. But he'd already offered himself, and been rudely refused. So I didn't suggest it.

Two weeks later, a tall, burly major strode into the office. Dottie, Buster and I came to attention. The major handed Dottie a calling card and asked her to present it to the colonel. Displaying her bodice to best advantage, Dottie passed it on to me. I read the words "Theodore M. Fritsche III, Major, United States Air Force," ran my eyes up and down the blue uniform, plastic nameplate and gold oak leaves, stopped at the face and recognized the ice-water eyes of the alpha who'd worked me over in the room with a view at the Uaddan Hotel.

I introduced myself using my real name. He gave no sign that we'd ever met. I'd played that game often enough myself but, I had to admit, never so well. He granted me not the slightest nod of recognition. In a voice as flat as a physics lecture he informed me that, as Ambassador Boardman's new military attaché, he was entitled to a secure, American-owned villa. The villa, however, was undergoing renovations. Until the work was complete, and for better security, he'd been advised to use the visiting officers' quarters at Wheelus rather than a hotel.

He handed me a set of orders signed by the ambassador's second secretary. Captains were sharing toilets at Wheelus. Nothing was being renovated. Our ground lease would be up in 1970 and the odds were good it would not be renewed. Majors were entitled to two-room suites and I knew that none was available. Although billeting was not my responsibility, it briefly crossed my mind that this particular major might consent to share a toilet with the executive aide. One glance at his unyielding eyes and thin, narrow mouth scotched that.

After a word with the colonel, I led him into the private office and closed the door behind him.

Jesus, fuck. He's not only not *an oil field roughneck, he's Air Force. How the hell am I going to handle this? I was sure I'd never see the bastard again. Now I may run into him every time I hit the gym or set foot inside the embassy.*

Fritsche exited the private office five minutes later, two paces behind the colonel. Swanson handed me a set of orders, endorsed by himself. "Taxi the major over to the housing office, Joe. Tell them to use the general officer's suite in the VOQ. We haven't had a general on base in six months." He glanced at the major. "If some general does fly in, you'll just have to bunk with Joe here. That OK? As you may not be aware, we're full up."

The major glanced at me as if I were a hat rack. "Hey, bud," he said, sticking out his hand. "The Colonel tells me you're one great guy. I also been told you play a mean game of tennis. Share quarters with you any time."

Share quarters? Yeah, right. Tennis? Where'd he get that? Ambassador Boardman? Talk about mixed signals.

Tennis and swimming at the Uaddan were the two sports that had bound her son and me together in a masculine, athletic but not overtly erotic friendship. It wasn't exactly common knowledge on base or, I presumed, at the embassy. There was no reason to suppose that Swanson knew anything about it.

Is Mama aware of the aborted holiday tryst? Is she craftily providing me with a tempting playmate, a muscular substitute for her weedy son?

"We got to get together, hear? I used to play tennis a lot."

I thought he'd wink but he didn't.

Maybe he has a twin. Maybe the roughneck that worked me over is his brother. Maybe this bull just sounds the same and looks the same. Maybe this one's happily married and hasn't touched a dick besides his own since high school. Maybe I was a lot drunker than I thought.

I looked at his hands. The wedding ring he wore was plain, dull gold, not carved and flashy. The wristwatch matched the ring. There was no ID bracelet.

Before we set off for housing, Major Fritsche treated all concerned to the pleasure of his company, asking Buster Wilson where he hailed from and where he'd served, and ogling Dottie Bacon more than masculine courtesy required. He wished the two of them goodbye with the remark that he'd been told on good authority that this office was a model of efficiency and military courtesy and that they were both damned lucky to serve under outstanding officers such as the colonel and myself.

Late that afternoon, I overheard a whispered exchange between the two clerks.

"Don't you even think about playing French maid at the VOQ, Peaches."

"Mind your bees-wax, Tubby. He looked at me real fine. Good looker himself. If you ask me."

"Some guys in my barracks, they look real good, too, I guess. Not married and younger than him. Real studs. You could help 'em out."

"You kidding? Why should I? They've got you and the soap and the showers for that."

"Bitch."

"At least I'm no lard ass."

A few days later, I asked Airman Wilson to pull together what information he could on Major Theodore M. Fritsche III. Lacking access to Pentagon or Department of the Air Force files, there wasn't much. His home of record was Bozeman, Montana. He came up through ROTC. Officially, his previous assignments had been Ramstein Air Base, Germany; Robins, in Georgia, and Guam, serving in either aircraft maintenance or administration. There was no record of assignment to a forward unit that had been wiped out. He was married with one child; his wife's name was given as Mary Ellen McBroom Fritsche, not Dorris, the name tattooed on the roughneck's arm.

Jeff and I met with Captain Harper the next week. On some occasions, even the bravest man needs a buddy's moral support.

Harper had heard from the legal officer at Little Rock Air Base. He'd interviewed the guilty Mrs. Jeff, taken her statement and eventually gotten her signatures on the court documents he'd prepared. Mrs. Jeff admitted her culpability, agreed to a no-fault divorce, signed a statement that Captain Jeff was not responsible for alimony or child support and that she would not ask for either, now or a later date. The baby would be put up for adoption. Jeff was free after signing several multi-layer documents that Captain Harper lay before him.

After he'd done so, Captain Harper tore off carbon copies of each, added them to a stack of papers, slipped them into an envelope and handed it to Jeff. "You'll need to run these through Personnel, Captain Masters. Get your allotments changed, maybe your next-of-kin form, insurance, all of that. Congratulations. You're a free man."

Jeff looked at the envelope as if it were a nest of snakes. "Yes, ma'am. Thank you, ma'am. I appreciate all you done for me. I sure do. You been real professional. For sure."

The crack in his voice and the exaggerated country-boy language said plainly that he was on the edge of bawling. I got him out of Harper's office and onto the street as fast as I could.

"The bitch. I loved her. The bitch. How could she do this to me? A baby. And I'll never see it. I wanted a son so bad, a little Jeff. Christ, Joe. I wanted a little son so bad."

After I made a couple of phone calls, we drove to Colonel Opstein's off-base villa. Mrs. Opstein, tall, slim and elegant in the way that her husband was solidly athletic and plain, greeted us as friends, showed us into a den and left us alone. The room was furnished with Libyan rugs, huge floor cushions, low chairs, hand-wrought lamps and a brass tray-table set with brandy, Jack Daniel's, soda water, ice, glasses, peanuts and a platter of cut-up fresh fruit.

Ops, who arrived a drink or two later, stood in for the deceitful Chaplain Jenner as counselor-in-chief. I minded the drinks and said as little as possible about Jeff's failings as a faithful husband and moral straight-arrow. Ops knew most of the damning details anyway. His power as a leader was that he accepted his men's mistakes and honored each of us for our best qualities.

Jeff had many such attributes: courage, physical strength, the inability to tell a lie, the determination to stand by a buddy and a superior officer whose moral and religious values were alien to his own. It took most of the night but we at least got Jeff on the road to admitting and accepting his guilt and shame. Working through these feelings to some sort of livable solution wasn't going to happen overnight, of course.

"I drove her to it, my dirty demands, asked her to do things no lady ought to do. Worthless fuck, that's what I am."

"You're a good man, Jeff-o. You got through Nam. You got decorated. You're tough. You're worth a hundred bumble-butt majors that won't ever make colonel."

"If she'da just come over, accompanied tour, three years. We could have had a villa, too. A maid to help her. I'd never have gotten mixed up with those rotten Libyan whores."

"It's hard on a younger man, Jeff-o. Military life. But you can handle it. Joe's not going to let you down. I'm not."

"Damn right," I put in, retrieving Jeff's empty glass and refilling it with JD and soda.

"Jeff-o, do you know who—?"

"No! And I don't want to. I'd kill the bastard maybe. Cut his fucking balls off, turn him into a steer."

We were sitting on floor pillows. Ops had his big arm around Jeff's shoulder. He was being as good to the grieving Jeff as Uncle Carl had often been to me. Too many men I'd known had treated other men badly—my drunken father, the tragic wingmen Conroy and Totenberg, the abusive surgeon I'd helped send to his death at the DMZ. This was the way men should be with each other, the best and wisest caring for their own.

"Jeff-o, Jeff-o, Jeff, it's OK for you to grieve. You're not perfect, nobody is. It'll take time but you'll forgive yourself, and we're with you on that, OK?"

"Yes sir. Only I love—loved—her, and I wanted a son. See, I was an orphan and adopted out. I wanted a family. I wanted my own son."

"And you can have a son, two, four, six sons. You've got sense in your head and lead in your pencil. Divorcing a cheating wife, that's the same as walking away from a chaplain who spills your private conversations to the OSI. Even if the regs allow it."

"I can't cry on you guys' shoulders night and day."

"And I'm not going to let you. We'll get you through this. You're our number one mission right now."

"I'm fucked. What the fuck am I—?"

Ops bear-hugged Jeff's head onto his shoulder. "I've been looking into this just a little. One thing does come to mind."

"Shoot the bitch and the bastard who did it to her and wronged me, one minute after I cut off his—"

Ops Dutch-rubbed Jeff's ear with his fist. "Fix me another drink, Joe. Jeff-o, listen up. You may not know that we have a non-denominational prayer and discussion group on base. It's for men who are away from their wives and families. It operates through the USO's recreation department, not the chaplain service.

"I'm not an alcoholic, sir. I know I been drinking too much lately but—"

"It's not AA. I want you to give it a try."

Jeff started crying again. "I need to go to the toilet, sir."

"Out the door, make a left. Tell me you'll think about it."

Jeff swabbed his face. "Colonel, you know I'll do anything you say."

"Except quit going to that house downtown?"

"I have stopped. That's for sure. Gotta pee now."

I handed Ops his drink. I decided not to tell him about the madam's warning that we'd been followed. It could wait.

Ops saluted me. Odd for a colonel to salute a captain. He explained quick enough.

"Thanks for bringing him here, son. Right away, before he did something foolish."

"Yes sir. Stupid-cop games, we call it."

Ops smiled. "You're the hero in this mess. You know how to call the right person to fix something that's broke. Reminds me of me fifteen years ago. You got him to the lawyer, you helped work this out at a distance—and without totally pissing him off. So far."

"We're buddies. We both helped out when the other got in trouble."

"I know that, Joe. This is different. I don't want to say you wouldn't understand but, well, wives, children—"

Cotton writhing in my bed in Switzerland, crying out in pain, my shame at hurting him, my fear of being exposed and punished, the two of us separated forever—all that jumped to mind.

"I understand it well enough, Colonel."

"He's going to be angry. At you, for getting involved, for knowing, for seeing him break down. No man wants to be embarrassed in front of his friend. Shame, resentment—some of it's going to spill over. Onto me, too. And God help Captain Harper if he ever needs her advice again."

"I understand that, sir."

"He might say things. This will not simply disappear overnight. Cut him some slack, son."

Homosexuals can't get married to each other. We can't have children. Thank you, Jesus.

With that in mind, I mixed myself a final drink and tried not to think about Cotton's upcoming Easter break, his eighteenth birthday two days ago or what his angry, self-righteous Papa might already have said or done.

CHAPTER 9

FLOWERS IN HIS HAIR

I'd sent Cotton a birthday card, of course, but no gift. Since Christmas, we'd exchanged a few very short, circumspect letters. They focused on trivialities such as the weather, sports and Cotton's required reading. After the nightmare rendezvous in Gstaad, we both knew better than to commit to paper anything that might be considered even vaguely objectionable by his parents, the OSI or some dirty-minded military censor.

Cotton was due to arrive in Tripoli on Sunday morning, April seventh, a week before Easter. He knocked on my BOQ door the day before that, about two p.m. His winter-white face was a long question mark, his sparse moustache perhaps a bit thicker and blonder than it had been in December. He seemed another inch taller.

"Surprise!"

I pulled him inside with one hand and shut the door with the other. I was delighted to have him not only by himself but a day early. Still, I couldn't forget where we were. "You bet your butt I'm surprised. Did anybody see you?"

"Just a local outside, sweeping the sidewalk."

"Good. How was your flight?"

"Hawk, I know we've got to be careful."

I couldn't help myself. "Our friendship. You still want to—?"

"I caught the earlier flight so we could do this. Luckily, Mama has talks at the prime minister's office all day today. I knew that from her last letter. Aren't you glad I'm here?"

I was scared to touch him, afraid of losing control a second time. "Do you forgive me, Crane?"

"For what?"

"Hurting you. Getting you in trouble with your father. Of course I'm glad you're here. Don't you know how often I think of you? How much? And I was hoping that last Christmas—aw, shit, kiddo. What a mess. I've been worried sick."

"About what else?"

"That we'd never see each other again. That your mother would have me arrested. All sorts of hell."

"God. Well, I'm here now. We've got ten days to swim and play tennis and do—stuff."

Cotton's presence was an answer of sorts but I wanted it in words as well as deeds. "Christmas should have been wonderful. And I fucked up big time. I'd saved up too much energy. I was thinking with the wrong end of my spine."

"Energy?"

"I'm watching my mouth, trying to be a gentleman around young Master Boardman. OK?"

"Quote: 'It is said that Socrates commits a crime by corrupting the young men and'—I don't remember you ever talking dirty to me."

"Balls, Plato. I was thinking with my big, hairy balls. Are you still OK with what we were going to do together?"

Cotton grinned wickedly, grabbed me around the waist and pulled me into what would be called a bear hug if brawnier bodies were involved. "Just us guys, Hawk—and then Papa butted in. Can we talk about that later? Are those doors locked?"

I checked. Both were locked. My briefs were getting tight, my pulse was pounding. I was damned if I'd botch this one.

Cotton didn't let me. The man he was growing into took charge. "Hawk, do you remember when we were out at Leptis Magna last summer, in the ruins?"

"You kidding? You said it was the most embarrassing moment of your life."

"And you said that, with any luck, it wouldn't be."

"You just got overheated. Me, too, but I had to hold back. I was the adult."

"I wish you hadn't. We wasted almost a year."

"We've got time now. At Leptis, we'd been looking at hard dicks all morning. Phalluses carved in stone. Naked statues. You couldn't control yourself. They call it raging teenage hormones."

"My dick has been hard since my plane left Rome," Cotton answered. "I want to play with your big hairy balls."

"I've never heard you talk dirty either."

"Do you recognize this shirt, Hawk? And the shorts?"

"Are you, is that what you wore out to the ruins that day? Cool."

"Don't worry, everything's been through the laundry. So I thought, um, well, I thought maybe we could play that scene again, start over from five minutes before I grabbed you."

My trousers were tented out. Anticipating Cotton's visit and hoping for the best, I hadn't gotten off in more than a week. I put my hands on his sides and began to lift his shirt.

"No, like we were at Leptis, dressed. Instead of getting naked all at once, like in Gstaad. This time, anyway."

He pulled me close and we started kissing, lips closed at first, but suddenly we were into each other like a couple of horny minks. Cotton's stiff erection bumped against mine and, when I started humping against him, he slipped his big right hand into the back of my pants and rubbed my tailbone.

"Lucky I had a shower this morning, Crane."

"You're going to need another one, you know?"

With Cotton taking the lead, we made love with our clothes on, standing up. From hugging and kissing, we progressed to passionate frottage, gentler groping, deeper kisses and an embrace so total that clothes ceased to exist.

He was right, I was going to need another shower. I didn't last long. I shot off without even removing my shoes, Cotton laughed when I lost control, gently stroking my fading erection until I begged him to stop. Unlike some similar incidents back in California, it didn't feel like gas-station sex. It felt like the beginning of a long, wonderful journey. It felt like love.

"Now me," he whispered when I started to recover. I pulled him close, kissed him some more, licked his ears and eyes and neck. When I put one hand inside his shirt and dropped the other down to the substantial lump in his shorts, he flinched. "Go slow, Joe. I'm all yours. Take your time."

I did go slow, touching him the way I like to be touched, the way I'd been touched by my first lover, the now-married preacher who'd been my freshman dorm counselor at Vanderbilt.

Cotton lasted longer than I did, though not by much. He was eighteen years old, his sex drive as high as it ever would be, his need for me apparently even more desperate than mine for him.

I didn't laugh when he came. I kissed him again, my eyes wide open, his the same, our locked-on stare better than the deepest kiss. He'd been right, my wise boy. Replaying the Leptis scene, this time successfully, erased the Gstaad fiasco. Our clothes didn't separate us. We were one man, sweaty, sopping wet and, for the moment, satisfied.

We just stood there for a couple of minutes, holding each other, breathing together. Finally, Cotton took a step back.

"OK, old man. Now you can take off my shirt."

"And the rest of it?"

"Will you lend me some clean underwear again? I'm still about your size."

I lifted his shirt, tossed it aside and touched his button-hard nipples. The dusting of cotton-white hair was thicker than it had been four months earlier. "Sure. But not right away. You on some kind of schedule?"

He unbuckled his belt. "We probably have another hour. Can you call me a taxi?"

I lowered his zipper and let his shorts drop. "You're a taxi. A wet taxi, a very messy taxi. The sexiest taxi I've ever had my hands on. These Jockeys are soaked."

"You're a card, Hawk. I believe you were driving. Let me get them off so I can take care of you."

I raised my arms. "Get to work, boy. Drive me crazy. In one hour, we can—"

"Yeah, we can, and this time on your bed. If that's OK."

"Anywhere you say, Crane.

"All places that the eye of heaven visits
"Are to a wise man ports and happy havens.
"Teach thy necessity to reason thus;
"There is no virtue like necessity."

"How long have you been out of school, Joe?"

"I didn't lose my memory in four years, Crane. I wish *Richard the Second* weren't so long.

"This royal throne of kings, this scepter'd isle,
"This earth of majesty, this seat of Mars,

"This other Eden, demi-paradise—"

"By Hollywood standards, they're all too long. What if we'd never found each other?

"Against the envy of less happy lands,
"This blessed plot, this earth, this realm, this England.

"Hawk, what if we were Chinese and didn't have Shakespeare?"

I drew back the coverlet and top sheet on the bed. "Confucius say, What if we were heterosexual?"

"I'd still love you. It wouldn't matter. The problems would just be different."

Single beds on military bases weren't designed to hold two Jack Beanstalks with broomstick arms and feet like shovels. Getting comfortable took a bit of experimentation. Cotton's erection never entirely subsided but, after a few welcome-back strokes and tugs, I kept my hands to myself. We needed to talk. With Cotton's head on my arm, his dick resting on my hip and his mouth close enough to occasionally kiss, we settled down and I popped the sixty-four-dollar question. "Here goes, Kiddo. What happened with your father after I left?"

Cotton took a deep breath before he answered. "Yeah, we have to talk about that. First he said I'd grow out of it, he did." Cotton's face twisted into a silent *yuck.* "I didn't even want to think about Papa doing—you know?"

"Conventional wisdom. Did he go to an all-boys school?"

"St. Paul's."

"So he understands the theory. Maybe he had a crush on a coach or upperclassman. It happens."

"This isn't a crush, I told you."

"I know. Same here."

"Anyway, by that night, back at the Palace Hotel, where he and Bunny were staying, he was raging, drinking. Said he was going to have your ass in jail, Mama back in divorce court and his precious but misguided son and heir back in the States under *his* watchful eye."

"It hasn't happened. He change his mind?"

I didn't like the threats involved. I started shivering so I pulled up the sheet to cover us.

"It comes and goes. On Christmas Day, he was all Santa Claus, gave me this Movado"—Cotton held up his hand to show a gold watch with a gold mesh band.

"We had turkey and plum pudding in the hotel dining room. Said I'd meet a nice girl one day, forget the dad-lad stuff when I got to college, marry, have children, the works."

"Quoth the Bard yet again: 'It is a wise father that knows his own child.'"

"When Papa opens his mouth it's more like an idiot, full of sound and fury, signifying nothing."

"Signifying that he can make a hell of a lot of trouble. Keep us separated until you're twenty-one, for instance. Send me to Leavenworth."

Cotton groaned. "Mama hates him. She knows I'm friends with you. We saved each other, kind of."

"No kind-of about it, Mister Hero." I touched his side and he gasped and wiggled like a stroked puppy. "So what's happening now?"

"A month ago, he wrote and all but ordered me to fly to Virginia for Easter, go to dances in Charlottesville and Washington, meet debutantes."

"Nice girls."

"Get them to a nunnery, I say. I refused. Mama backed me up."

That sounded better. I put my arm around Cotton's neck and pulled him closer. "The race riots in Washington and Baltimore probably cancelled most of the deb parties. I'm not supposed to say this, but when the word came in about Reverend King's murder, my boss made us draw up a contingency plan. He was ordered to by USAFE."

"More likely it could happen in Vietnam. The *Herald Tribune* ran pictures of soldiers with peace symbols on chains around their necks. Like the one you wore last spring. One Marine grunt had it stenciled on his helmet. He was black."

"I still have it. Hand me my Bermudas, will you, please?" Cotton fished a couple of clippings out of the back pocket. The first, from *Newsweek*, was an illustrated article about a huge anti-war march in San Francisco. The second, from a grocery store tabloid, showed two long-haired men holding hands at an outdoor concert by the rock group Jefferson Airplane. They were naked.

"Why don't you quit the Air Force, Joe? I'll quit school. We can run away to California. You can let your hair grow out. We can wear flowers and be hippies together."

This was unrealistic but appealing. I hesitated before saying, quietly, "There's a war on, Crane. Didn't anybody tell you? Hawk's got a commitment."

"President Johnson's dropped out of the presidential race because of all the peace marches. Senator McCarthy won the Wisconsin Democratic primary last Tuesday as a peace candidate. The war's going to be over."

"Some day it will. I'd like to show you the San Francisco I love—North Beach, the Presidio, Golden Gate, City Lights bookstore."

"And we could go to concerts and hold hands?"

I thought I'd better change the subject. After kissing his shoulder and noting that he smelled like a man, not a boy, I returned to the main matter at hand.

"Does your mother know about Gstaad? What did he tell her? Is she on the warpath?"

"She knows about the surprise visit but not that he caught us together."

My mouth moved from his shoulder to his lips. "Good. That's good to hear."

"There's another reason I wanted to see you before you—before we—saw her. Them."

"Them? Does that mean, 'however?'"

"Papa consulted his lawyer. He's flying in here tomorrow for a showdown with Mama. He's going to charge Mama with lack of oversight concerning my moral education and ask the court for joint custody. If she doesn't agree right away, he's going to demand that she initiate charges against you for corruption of an innocent, underage boy, dishonorable conduct, sodomy, the whole nine yards."

My balls suddenly clenched tight against my ass. "He forced you to tell him what happened?"

"Joe!"

I kissed him again. "No, you wouldn't have said anything."

"He actually phoned me with all this. They called me out of class. It's not like he didn't know about Qamar, the tennis player in Delhi. Mama told him something. She has sole custody, but he has to agree to stuff like changing schools. Or he did when I was a minor."

"Happy eighteen, by the way."

"And you're my present."

I moved my hand up his chest, fiddling with one of his erect nipples before he pushed my hand away. "We're *exchanging* presents. Like we didn't get to do last Christmas."

I was putting on a brave face but I was suddenly terrified. I felt like a schoolboy caught cheating on an exam or jerking off in the library. "Maybe it's a mistake for you to even be here now. Maybe—"

"Maybe you're going to trust me to deal with Mama. I'm going to make her see how serious we are about staying together and loving each other."

"Jesus, Crane. You're the ballsiest kid I ever met."

"It's what I want. I'll play the boarding school game just so long as she agrees that we can get together occasionally and without interference from Papa."

I put my other arm around him and pulled him tight. He had courage enough for both of us.

"Is that what you want, too, Joe. Just us guys?"

"Of course it is. But she's going to explode. She's not going to listen. You're in school. I'm in the military. We should have waited. I take full responsibility."

This was a thoughtless thing to say after what we'd just shared, cruel and stupid. The encounter at the Uaddan with the alpha who turned out to be Ted Fritsche popped into my mind. Having dominated and used me, he'd thrown me out. Nothing was shared. And I not only hadn't minded, I'd wondered whether I needed such a man rather than a compliant youth. But this was no boy in bed with me. This was a wise and clever, younger man. Cotton had walked in and taken charge. That he was maturing into my equal was somehow reassuring.

Extricating himself from the embrace, Cotton climbed out of bed, struck a heroic pose—a marble statue sprung from antiquity, a warrior holding a shield—and mock-declaimed "We're Achilles and Patroclus." Naked, and sounding as serious as he'd ever been, the simile fit. As a boy he'd proved himself a hero when the embassy was attacked. Now he was old enough to be drafted, if not to buy a beer in most of the U.S., much less vote. For a moment, he almost had me convinced. "Sacred brothers, a band of two," he added. "Like in Thebes."

"I don't think your parents want to hear about ritualized pederasty in Ancient Greece."

"You're coming to dinner at the embassy tomorrow night, right?"

"Roger. But your father can't use you and me as entertainment at a diplomatic reception."

"They hate each other, like I said. He's leaving Bunny back in Virginia. It's dinner for four."

"With my head on a platter."

"Not if I can help it. I think she'll see it my way." He dropped the shield. A determined young man stood before me, visibly aroused and breathing hard. "I have a couple of arguments she'll listen to, if I have to use them. Nothing to do with you."

I gestured at his midsection. "But that secret weapon does? Have to do with me?"

"Can't help it, Captain Hawk. Yeah. You're the target "

I threw off the sheet, swung around and put my feet on the floor. He knelt before me and sniffed. "You smell like Gorgonzola, kind of."

"What's that?"

"Italian blue cheese."

"Do you like Gorgonzola?"

"I do now."

"You think you're so—Christ, where'd you learn to do that?" I touched his ears. He shook his head and kept at what he was doing. "Boarding school? They teach this stuff at Le Rosey?"

He leaned back. "It's my last year. I took an advanced course."

I pulled his face toward mine. "Wise guy."

He kissed me back, deep and hard, tongues wrestling, and then pulled loose. "If I'm going to graduate with honors—"

I kissed his nose. "This whole spring break, you're getting tutored."

"Yes, Captain Hawk. Assuming we get through the showdown with Papa and Mama alive."

"Back to work, Master Crane. You're doing A-OK so far."

He spread my knees wider with his big, flame-scared hands. I loved those hands, loved the fact of him touching me with them, loved them even more than what he was doing with his mouth.

"You know I love you more than my own life, Crane?"

He cocked his head to one side, serious as a terrier begging a treat. "You'd better. Because it goes double for me."

"Just us guys?"

He nodded. "For sure."

Happiness has its price. Jeff spotted us leaving the BOQ. He confronted me later that night. His anger almost matched the raging outbursts aimed at his wife and whoever fathered her child.

"You fucker, you promised me not to throw your, your—sex life—in my face. That time I had to look at you naked, getting reamed out like a pig by a sergeant. You said you'd either quit it or take it off base. God damn you."

Ops's prediction had come true. Jeff's fury was out of all reason. I tried a lie but he wasn't listening.

"You don't know what we—"

"This is a new low, Joe. It's disgusting, not only a kid but the kid you saved and that saved you in that bottle-bomb attack. Does he even shave yet? Are you crazy, don't you know this is probably statutory rape? God damn you to Hell."

He hadn't hit his wife so I was fairly certain he wouldn't start pounding on me. "He's eighteen."

"He's a kid. His mom would turn you into a set of Nazi lampshades."

"Calm down, Jeff."

"No. This time, you could be involving me. Agent Bivens might start lumping Jeff-o together with all you fucking bachelors—Muscles Denman, your stud-horse medic, those fliers that bought the farm. Well, I ain't having any of it, you hear me?"

For the second time that day, I managed to change the subject. "What about Bivens?"

"He called me in again. I'm not supposed to talk about it."

"He heard about Rae Connolly looking into her brother's murder?"

"Keep going."

"You swore you wouldn't say anything?"

"And I'm not, not this time."

Shit, I thought, my heart suddenly racing. *Has loving Cotton wrecked not only my career but my friendship with Jeff? Am I headed for a court martial?*

I thought fast. "He told you to back off, that you were operating way above your pay grade, you and your buddy the beanstalk?"

He ducked his head. "And Muscles. All of us. Is he a homo, too, by the way?"

"By the way, I never said a word about how you got your butt cut that time. The whore with the whip, Renata, she got deported. You remember?"

"This is a whole nother ball game. We're talking a lot worse than discipline and leather work."

I cut him off. "Let's go see Ops on Monday. I don't think Bivens has any business sticking his nose into this. Why did you include Major Denman? Did Bivens ask about him again?"

"Can't say, Joe, like I said. Sure, let's go see Ops on Monday. We can talk on the track. Ops has got to outrank Bivens."

"You're not going to mention—?"

"Not this time. I owe you. But keep the kid out of here. Hear me? O.U.T. Out."

And so we had a trade-off, a truce. Bent in opposite directions, Jeff and I were both trapped in webs of fear, desire, anger and secrecy. Despite my ability to work the system, I was badly shaken after getting caught with Cotton a second time. Jeff, an evangelical Christian by upbringing and belief, had exploded in moralistic righteousness after yet another betrayal of promises by someone he'd trusted.

I wondered if I could count on him in a showdown with Bivens or, for that matter, the Boardmans. I had to admit I didn't know. He was my buddy, and I just didn't know. For a military man, that's one very dangerous situation.

Winston Boardman arrived in Tripoli on schedule, checked into the Uaddan Hotel and presented himself right on time for the scheduled dinner at the embassy. Tall and conventionally better looking than either his ex-wife or son, he turned out to be verbally facile but comparatively stupid. As a former undercover agent, he was well-schooled in purposeful vagueness and social niceties. Rather than saying, for instance, "Yes, we've met" when we shook hands—naturally leading to where and when and why—he did the "Oh, yes, of course" routine and I did the same. Up to this point, Elizabeth wasn't aware of the interrupted tryst in Gstaad. Winston was happy to let Cotton and me stew during the meal, while the butler Ma'amoud and other servants were present. But over coffee, as if gossiping about a powerful politician caught in bed with a socialite's daughter, he shared with Elizabeth his overblown tale of surprising Cotton and me practically *in flagrante*.

"Our son was sitting on the unmade bed, his sweater and shoes on the floor." He glanced in my direction. "This one was packing, trying to get away. You, sir, must have known how small a town is Gstaad. Someone would have reported you to the authorities if I hadn't turned up."

"I know it looked bad," I said, interrupting as he described the disordered double bed at length. "But nothing much happened. Kid stuff."

I hoped the lie would pass muster. My intended act of love had been side-tracked into near rape by thoughtlessness and out-of-control desire. After our session yesterday, I was sure Cotton wouldn't contradict me.

"God knows," Boardman said, turning to his ex-wife, "what they'd been up to before I got there to set things straight. In Switzerland," he continued, "the age of consent for any such unnatural behavior is twenty."

At this point Ambassador Boardman did a surprising thing. Rather than listen to more, she rang for Ma'amoud. "Show Mr. Boardman to the library. Bring him brandy and a cigar. We'll join him in a moment."

Dismissed, Boardman rose, bowed, muttered "I'm not through with this, Lizzie," and followed the servant out.

When the three of us were alone, she continued. "Kid stuff? However it looked, you, sir, are no kid."

"No, ma'am."

"My boy was seventeen last Christmas?"

"I believe so. Yes, ma'am."

Her rage was more controlled than Jeff's but potentially as lethal. "You believe so? It may be kid stuff to you but, believe me, my child is all I have in the world. And you, sir, you led me to believe you planned to marry one day—and now this? Leading my innocent child astray? Why should I believe a word you say, ever again?"

Cotton coughed and broke in, his voice veering up, then down. "Joe knows about my friend in Delhi, Mama."

"Now that indeed was kid stuff. You're impressionable and too impulsive. He was older, already perverted, ruined. You're not—not one of, of those. You'll change."

"Papa knows, too."

"The bare minimum. To get you out of Delhi and into Le Rosey."

"He knows the whole story. I told him at Christmas. He said it was disgusting what we'd done."

Cotton's face was red, his voice now under control.

"Well, it was. Unnatural. Unspeakable. Nice people—"

"Nice people can love other people. Especially heroes. Joe saved my life and I saved his. We belong to each other."

There, it was out. In her genteel world, what we'd shared the day before was unspeakable. I was looking at a stretch in Fort Leavenworth.

Mrs. Boardman turned to me. "Captain Harding, I'm afraid you're going to have to consider the consequences of this very grave, very serious lack of good judgment. This moral lapse. An insult not only to me and my son but to the uniform you wear. Under the circumstances—"

Cotton suddenly slugged down half a glass of wine. "If we're going to ruin a career or two, what about you and Colonel Swanson? He's basically your subordinate, right? Your inferior. And you meet him at the Uaddan. In a room, a suite. He's been here alone, upstairs. I could open my mouth."

"How dare you? How dare you? Who told you that?"

Cotton had suddenly leveled the field. By not denying the charge, she'd confirmed it.

"A little bird."

"Someone here, in the embassy? I'll bust him down to GS3. He'll go home in chains. He can share a cell with—" She gestured at me.

"A little dead bird."

"Ferrette? He was funny that way, wasn't he? Did he try to interfere with you, say improper things to get your attention?"

The *yuck* expression again. "I don't know. He was old, disgusting. He did let me know he was agency. I was supposed to be impressed."

"Be quiet. Captain Harding isn't—"

"Ma'am, everybody knew he was agency. Sexually? If I had to guess—"

"You don't have to guess, Captain. Be quiet. I will settle this matter with Cotton's father. I believe he is capable of listening to reason."

Had we won a grudging acceptance? Or had Cotton's blackmail attempt succeeded? I wasn't sure. My hands were shaking so I kept them under the table, as young officers are trained to do.

Mrs. Boardman turned to Cotton. "You will be leaving for Switzerland tomorrow morning."

"Mama, I'm supposed to be here ten days. Vacation isn't over yet."

"It is for you, sweetheart. You talk too much. And I need time to think— think and discuss the matter with your Papa."

"We're—Joe and I—Ma'amoud's supposed to drive us out to Sabratha, to see the ruins."

"That can wait until summer. Sabratha's been in existence almost two thousand years. A few more months won't matter."

At least she didn't say never.

"I want—we ..."

"Captain Harding, why don't you and Cotton withdraw to the small salon for a few minutes. Then I'm afraid you'll have to say your good-byes. Son, you must pack tonight." She rang the bell for Ma'amoud. "Telephone Jackie, please. Tell her to change Cotton's plane reservation. He needs to fly out tomorrow. Ask her to call Alitalia, will you? Tell her to call through to Rome if she must. And then usher Captain Harding out."

In the salon, Cotton and I sat opposite each other, both out of breath, unsure what would happen next. I'd only seen this look of utter desperation on his face twice before. Those had been about sex, and the lack of it. This was about love, and our sudden separation—possibly for a long, long time.

Finally, instead of talking about us, Cotton returned to the dead CIA agent, Pete Ferrette. "I might as well spill some more state secrets, you think?"

"Probably not."

"Fuck it. First of all, Mr. Ferrette didn't tell me about Colonel Swanson. I picked that up from—" he pointed toward the dining room and mouthed the word, *Ma'amoud.* "Kitchen gossip. Everybody knows what they've been doing."

For a schoolboy, Cotton was becoming a very convincing liar. His mother, no fool, had bought his story whole. He was already learning the necessity of cover-up in a dangerously prejudiced and moralistic culture.

"Protecting your source?"

"Wouldn't you?"

"She phones him at the office," I said. "We saw them at a table for two at the Swan. I believe he calls her Honeycakes."

"Gross."

"Is this room bugged?"

"Probably. I don't care. Mr. Ferrette said all kinds of things. I'll bet he was— you know. He tried to be friends, talked about getting laid but never mentioned any women."

"You could be right. That was my guess. But you didn't—?" I let the question hang.

Another *yuck* look. "Nooo. I didn't want anybody but you know who."

Presumably the room *was* bugged.

"He was running some kind of operation in and out of Wheelus, Joe. The Brits were involved somehow."

This all but confirmed Ferrette's connection to the mortars. But it didn't explain why he was the only fatality on a plane destroyed by another such shipment. Had he been killed or knocked out as the C-130 rolled down the runway? Was the whole thing a very expensive cover-up? Or were the botched takeoff and Ferrette's death purely coincidental?

"And he's dead," Cotton continued. "Did that have something to do with why you got ordered back at Christmas?"

I held up my hand in the universally recognized halt signal. Ferrette had clearly been indiscreet. Given the stakes, that alone could have been enough to doom him. If the room were indeed bugged, any further discussion was dangerous. The last things Cotton needed to know about were contraband weapons and two officers presumably terminated with extreme prejudice. There was no certainty I'd ever see the boy again.

Cotton got it. "OK."

I held up both hands and shrugged. Cotton got that, too—that I didn't know the answer to his question.

Leaning forward, Cotton whispered, "Can we write?"

I nodded and stood. "Be careful. I'd better get going. I'll miss you, kiddo. You know that."

Cotton stood too, very close. We didn't touch. Tears rolled down his face but he wasn't sobbing. I could feel his breath. "Goes double for me. Only damn Ferrette, damn Papa, double-damn—"

I gave him another halt sign, a big smile and then as jaunty a salute as I could manage. "We'll get through it, Patroclus. This ain't Troy."

He nodded solemnly and returned the salute. "Yeah, Achilles, I think we will. Just us guys. Come on world. We can take it."

Cotton was a brave, ballsy young man. But at that moment I had doubts, very serious doubts that we could.

I didn't fall apart until I got back to my room, stripped and sank down on the bed. The pillow smelled like Cotton. I wrapped my arms around it, kissed it half a dozen times and finally began to cry.

PART TWO

CHAPTER 10

LOVE LETTERS STRAIGHT

FROM THE HEART

*D*ear Joe,
I miss you so terribly and have so much to share with you. I know it's been little more than two months since we were together but it seems like ages. Do you miss me, too, honey? I can't go on without seeing you again. We need to make plans but you know me—I just hate letters and long-distance phone calls. Can we possibly spend a few days together, either the last weekend of this month or the first weekend of next? Madrid or Rome would be ideal because there are non-stop flights.

Say you will, darling. I know you can slip away if you really want to.

Pretty please. Wire me the date and name of the hotel. I'll be there with bells on.

Love, love, love,

Rae

After reading the letter, Jeff whistled. "Unless you were screwing this kitten while I wasn't looking, she's dug up something big."

"Yeah, that's what I think. Information she can't put on paper. She won't even trust a secure Pentagon phone. The return address is a P.O. box in Alexandria."

"Have we got enough good stuff to trade?"

It was time to fill Jeff in on the carbon flimsies and copies in my office safe.

After I told him, he whistled again. "Intelligence to spare. So what are you going to do?"

"I've never seen Rome. Hal Denman found a clean, cheap hotel near St. Peter's, with a good restaurant on the same block. I haven't taken but three days' leave since I got here. There's nothing on the books that's not numb-nuts routine."

Colonel Swanson told me to take as much time as I wanted, up to a week, for my Roman holiday. Leaving the office half an hour early, I taxied over to American Express, reserved flights and two single rooms in Rome, and sent this wire to Rae:

> *HONEYCAKES STOP YES YES YES STOP HOTEL ARCH-*
> *ANGELO ROME THURSDAY TWENTYFIFTH STOP PAS-*
> *SIONATE KISSES STOP JOE*

The buttery, cheesy fettuccine Alfredo at the Trattoria della Papa on Via Boezio was even richer than the Swan's version. The house white was smoother and cheaper. The dining room was quiet, candle-lit and didn't get busy until long after Rae and I finished supper.

And Rae, in civvies and on neutral ground, was a lot easier to deal with.

"Mama cried," she said. "When I showed her the letters you actually did draft about Ron—for the colonel's signature? Daddy went in their bedroom and shut the door. Eileen—that's my sister-in-law, Ron's widow—she got so tooth-spitting furious she practically screamed at me. 'Somebody played Ron for a fool and killed him and that was bad enough,' Eileen was yelling. 'Somebody military, in the government. And then they all turned around and thumbed their noses at us.'"

"I'm not disagreeing with you, ma'am. Or her. But not all of us."

"You want to make bird colonel or general as bad as I do, don't you, Joe?"

"Yes, ma'am. I won't deny it."

"Cut the ma'am. Call me 'Rae.'"

"Yes, Major. I mean Rae."

"So you do agree that the military—the branch of government we're devoting our lives to—may be responsible for my brother's murder?"

"Some unit within the military that's working with the Company—the Agency, yes, that's what it looks like to me."

"Keep talking, Joe."

"Or maybe some tin-star posse or off-the-books operation out of State, Special Forces cowboys paying off somebody else's debt. Could be bad guys working freelance."

"But the government, our government?"

"There's people that think the Mob paid the CIA to recruit and train James Harvey Oswald, brainwash him into a mental robot, and kill Kennedy. Jack Ruby, too."

"*The Manchurian Candidate.* Don't get me started. I'll blow my top. What it comes down to is that some nameless operatives we can't yet identify not only used and terminated Ron, they're going to use the power of the government to keep anybody from finding out what happened."

"That's about it. Only, as it also happens, we know stuff they don't know we know."

"Yeah, Joe, I think we do. But you have information I don't have and I've turned over a few stones myself. Still, I need to work this through more sources than just you and your brig-chaser buddy. And I will keep doing it."

"Right. Solving crimes committed on foreign soil, off base, is not in my job description. And Jeff and the local cops were bypassed like hitchhikers on the highway. Do you trust me to help you now?"

"Let me be frank. I've got fifteen years in and I distrust male career officers as a class. I've never had a less than perfect performance evaluation. My father was a radar tech in the Navy and retired from Motorola. He taught me how to do a man's work—and I do it. To get where I am, I've had to kick twice as much ass and volunteer for twice as many duty weekends as most of that Parris Island lumber I came up with." She sipped grappa and finished the thought. "The kind of limp dicks that spend half their time in the gym and the other half making excuses. I've sat through every pussy joke and farmer's-daughter story in the book. If I had two balls—"

"I'm glad I wore my steel jockstrap, Rae."

"It's nothing personal, Joe. You don't have what I call testosterone poisoning, or nothing like that Colonel Swanson of yours."

"What about General McAddams—who I've talked to on the phone but never met?"

"Funny case, McAddams. My ex-husband—"

"And his wife, school together, right. He flew with my buddy, Hal Denman, major in charge of Personnel, and helped me out with some reassignments."

"Yes. So you'll remember that I contacted the general soon after my brother visited me in November, and again when I returned from Wheelus. I gather he stays in very close touch with several of his former crew members."

"That's my impression." Rae Connolly was the last person on earth I'd tell about my relationship with Hal.

"They operate as a sort of old-boys network, relaying messages, helping each other out."

"Buddies do that." I didn't like where this was going.

"From what he said when we last talked, there are two of them at Wheelus right now, your friend Denman and another—another flyer."

I wasn't thinking clearly. The wine and a second grappa had dulled my brain. "Not the new motor pool officer, then. He's a fat Mormon and didn't fly."

"Some of them are more than buddies. I'm guessing here. Elmo McAddams considers himself slicker than a shit-house rat. But his wife can be dangerously indiscreet."

"Loose lips sink ships."

"She's not stupid. But half the Pentagon seems to know she sleeps upstairs and he runs all-male, all-night poker parties in the basement."

"Soldiers have been playing poker since Napoleon was a corporal."

"In Georgetown, couples stopped renting out finished basements to commissioned officers at the end of the Korean War. Your prize fighter was only one of many such bachelor officers. She finally put a stop to it."

Oh shit, she has Hal's number. "I had no idea—no idea the general was married or not married until you mentioned it in Tripoli."

"It was easy to put together, really. The pug, your buddy at Wheelus, he rented the basement for a couple of years. You'd better watch yourself. He takes orders from McAddams."

Have I flown all the way to Rome just to be run over by a lady Marine driving a halftrack? I need a clear head.

"How about we take this up tomorrow, Rae. It's been a long day. And you just flew in overnight."

She didn't hear me or didn't want to. "McAddams is at least bisexual. Certainly he's more than casually involved with one or both men at Wheelus. I took it

slow but I did ask him about the second man. I don't yet know his name. When I
sounded out Major Denman in February it also went nowhere."

"Hal's in the dark as far as your brother's concerned." I stood up. "I'm dead on
my feet. Good thing the hotel's so close. You ready?"

"General McAddams didn't answer me. Instead, he started off on some story
about his wife's brother. It was clear he was shutting me out. I don't trust him anymore, either personally or as a source."

Oh, fuck, how am I going to tell Hal about this?

"They serve coffee and rolls at the hotel starting at seven, Rae."

"I'm going to early mass at St. Peter's. Chance of a lifetime. Do you want me
to pray for you?"

"No. I'm good. Pray to your brother. Ask him to help us fix this."

"It doesn't work that way."

"It should."

"I'll knock on your door when I get back."

We threw coins over our shoulders at the Trevi fountain, ate gelato around the
corner from the Spanish steps, signed our names in the visitors' book at the Pan-
theon and shuddered at the thought of being torn apart by lions in the Coliseum.
Rae dipped holy water and genuflected inside at least a dozen churches and crossed
herself as we passed a dozen more.

Mostly we walked, talked, discussed possibilities and scenarios, let our res-
ervations, sadness and anger off the leash, and got to trust each other a bit more.

"I had to call in a few chits," Rae summed up over coffee in a bar near the hotel
late on Saturday. "Added to what I got from the general, the stories my brother told
me and my field work on your turf, I was able to access some very choice Marine
Intelligence background files." She took a slip of paper out of her purse and handed
it to me. "Ever heard of these guys?"

Four words were printed on the slip: Islamic Brotherhood Sharia Brigade. I
shook my head.

"It's an anti-royalist revolutionary group," she continued. "Operating out of
Tripoli."

"The underground's not my department. I have to assume there are dozens of
splinter groups wanting to replace the king, kick the Yank and Brit oppressors out
of Libya and take over the oil fields themselves."

"This group is known to have received mortars, shells and other weapons from the British, through an intermediary."

"That would be the guys that used your brother?"

"That would be the guys that killed my brother, yes."

"And they bit the hand that fed them."

"Pardon?"

I described the attack on the Royal Army detachment at Idris Airport.

"I didn't know about that. It doesn't make sense."

"Target practice, we think."

"We—meaning who?"

"I can't be specific. Diplomatic circles."

"I'm told your connections are good, Joe."

I shrugged modestly. "It's not who you know—"

"I wasn't able to put my hands on the name of a local contact, much less a membership list, if such a thing even exists."

"Jeff can check 'em out. Somebody received the weapons your brother was forced to ferry into town. We know the weapons came in on a regular Air Force service between Dover and Korat Air Base, Thailand."

"We do?"

I described in loose detail the carbon flimsies and copies of the flight plan and manifests stashed in my office safe.

"Keep talking, Joe. This is all fitting together."

"Jeff and I, we guess that the weapons offloaded in Tripoli were diverted from shipments intended for units in Southeast Asia."

"That's good. Use the unsuspecting motor pool officer to transport the contraband off base."

"So we figure there's got to be a Langley connection. Have you come across an agent named Pete Ferrette?"

"Company?"

"Tripoli station chief. Apparently unreliable, to my personal knowledge, indiscreet. Died when one of the C-130s crashed on takeoff at Wheelus."

"Terminated?"

"That's what Jeff and I think."

"By the man with the bloody face—that thought he recognized my brother?"

"That's the one. Anyway, Ferrette disappeared. There was a cover story about a heart attack while he was home on leave. What it looks like, though, is that his body was picked up and flown back the same way your brother's was. No finger-prints. No local investigation."

Rae took a pencil and a second slip of paper out of her purse.

"Pierre Ferrette," I said. "Middle initial L. He's since been replaced—at least this is my hunch—by an Air Force guy named Fritsche, Theodore M, the third, goes by Ted. He's attaché at the embassy but bunks in the Wheelus VOQ."

She kept writing.

"That may not be his real name, or he may have his own cover story."

"Everybody in this has a cover story, Joe."

She didn't have to tell me. And I sure wasn't going to give her the complete version of how and why I knew so much about the man who called himself Jay in civvies and Ted in blues.

"First time I met him he was drunk out of his mind, told me his whole unit had been taken out somewhere in Southeast Asia. He said he'd been on leave when his buddies were slaughtered, lost track of time, thought he might be AWOL. Used an-other name. Wasn't in control of himself, though it took me a while to see it. Later he sobered up and changed his story. Said he was oil company. When he reported in as Major Fritsche, I had him checked out, and it didn't."

"Didn't check out?"

"Not from the records I could access. I have a clerk who's pretty good with document trails."

"Let me see what I can do back in Washington."

"That's what I hoped you'd say."

Rae waved at the bartender. "Another brandy and soda, double."

"*Due*," I called. I'd started picking up restaurant Italian in Tripoli.

"Joe, I blame myself. I should never have let Ron join the frigging air farce, pardon my French."

"It didn't work this way in SAC. Most of the regs don't seem to apply at Wheelus."

"If he'd joined the Corps like I told him, I could have protected him."

"Not from this."

The bartender set down two highballs. Rae picked hers up and downed half in two gulps. "From me, my big mouth. I told frigging McAddams almost everything Ron told me in November—grand theft, intrigue, forced disregard of good order and discipline. McAddams sure as hell told somebody else. The wrong somebody else as far as my brother was concerned."

"You can't blame—"

"Cocksucking prick bastard isn't going to get away with it. Killing my baby brother that I diapered and burped. I'll take him to the OSI myself. I'll get the two-faced fudge-packer busted down breaking rocks as an airman basic."

I believed her. And the thought turned my balls stone cold. If McAddams went down, he'd likely take his younger buddies with him.

I've got to tell Hal. No, wait, Hal can't do anything about it. He might panic. He'll want to warn his daddy McAddams. That could doom Rae. And me. And probably Jeff. What the fuck are we going to do?

A day or two after my flight back from Rome, Colonel Swanson returned to the office following lunch off base. Airman Dottie Bacon was taking dictation from me—changes to the agenda for an upcoming staff meeting. Airman Wilson was filing sets of classified directives with one hand and eating a glazed donut with the other. A second donut lay on a plate on his desk.

Soundlessly strolling up behind Wilson, Swanson halted and barked, "When did you pass your last fitness test, Airman? Looks to me like you're taking more donuts than exercise."

Wilson jumped and almost dropped the donut. His mouth was full. "Sher?" He turned, chewed fast and swallowed.

Swanson slapped his own tight belly. "See this? I haven't added but an inch to my waist since West Point. You got to exercise, boy. And lay off the pogey bait."

"Had to work right through lunch, sir, and—"

"Look at your boss here. The captain's lean as a one-eyed snake. He works out—what is it, Joe? Four times a week?"

"At least, sir. Yes." *Jesus, why is the old man attacking Wilson? He's highly trained, skilled at his job and far leaner than the herds of tubby master sergeants and lieutenant colonels sucking up three government-subsidized meals a day at the mess hall, snack bar and clubs.*

"You better counsel your man, then. One more donut and he's liable to pop the buttons on his blouse."

Wilson's face had flushed red. He was deeply embarrassed, as was I. Swanson's remarks were needlessly cruel and way out of line. He might have taken me aside to make his point or even dropped me a short memo. Instead, he'd turned what should have been a mild and private correction into a humiliating spectacle.

After Swanson continued into his office and closed the door, Dottie Bacon picked up the untouched donut, took a dainty bite, chewed thoughtfully, and said, "The old meanie. That was just terrible. I think you look fine."

Wilson dropped his unfinished pastry into the trash. "He's right. I have a sweet tooth. But, God, what does it matter to him? My specialty code is clerk-typist, not Green Beret."

Dottie glanced at me, then back at Buster Wilson. "We're a dime a dozen, big boy. Like slaves or something. He don't care about enlisteds. But you know what?" She dropped the filched donut into the trash, cocked her hip, continued, "Old meanie treated little Peaches real bad, too. And she ain't forgetting it. You ain't either. Right?"

The angry female slave had not only decided it was pay-back time, she'd found a potential fellow rebel. Wilson stared at me, seeking direction.

She should have bitten it off when she had the chance, I thought. *Would've served the abusive old bastard right.* Instead, checking my Bulova, I shrugged and said, "The chow hall's still open. Why don't you guys take off and grab lunch?"

Wilson grinned. "You want ice cream, Boss?"

"Sure, why not, Buster? Ice cream is good. Even banana."

After work, I checked my mail box. Among several items, there was an envelope containing a greeting card. Sent airmail from Alexandria, Virginia, there was no return address. The single-fold card's cover was a familiar cinematic image: the airport scene in *Casablanca*, with club owner Rick and the compromised Captain Renault walking away from the camera. Inside, the printed greeting quoted the movie, "*The beginning of a beautiful friendship.*" Enclosed were four pieces of paper: two wallet-size photographs—Colonel Mark Earl Swanson's official portrait, flags included, and a studio shot of a much younger Lieutenant Fritsche wearing Army tans; a three-page carbon copy of Swanson's duty stations, TDYs as well as permanent changes of station; and a three-by-five-inch index card on which, written in blue crayon, were the words "Got a match?"

Swanson had served at Anderson, Guam. Fritsche's available records stated that he had as well. But Rae Connolly's puzzle package clearly meant more than that. And she'd become wary enough to use neither the Pentagon scramble phone nor her name and address.

I found Jeff in the O club bar, walked him outside and showed him the coded package.

"Damned if I know," he finally said. "She's onto something she doesn't want to say. Playing fucking mind games, you ask me."

"Her baby brother didn't protect himself. Look what it got him. She's being careful."

Jeff pulled a pack of cigarillos out of his pocket, lit one and inhaled. "That lard ass clerk you got. You're all the time bragging about how good he massages documents and top-secret shit. Give him something to do."

"Man, I can't tell him all the rest of it."

"Why would you do that? What Rae Connolly's saying is look at the records, see if they match."

"Match, match, match! Top cop, you are a fucking genius. I'll detail Airman Wilson first thing in the morning. Colonel's scheduled out to the bomb range the next two days."

"Into the air, junior birdman."

"What are you drinking, Top Cop?"

"Jack-in-the-Black, if you're buying."

"Doubles. With rib eye steaks on the side."

Three weeks later, I accompanied Jeff to a royal police sub-station on the south side of Tripoli. Jeff's counterpart greeted us with sweet mint tea and a typed, two-page confession that so far remained unsigned.

"We are not satisfied, my young sirs. We believe this man knows more he is not saying about."

A sadeek on the other side of a one-way mirror was strapped to a chair in a small, brightly lit interrogation room. He was wearing only urine-stained briefs. His head had fallen forward and he seemed to be asleep.

The royal police believed him to be a member, perhaps even a leader, of the Islamist brigade. Armed with a copy of the slip of paper given to me by Rae Connolly, Jeff had contacted the police chief a few days after my return from Rome. As we'd decided beforehand, he bypassed Colonel Swanson, Colonel Opstein and the embassy. The locals, informed that this tip came from an anonymous source high up in Washington, began a vigorous undercover investigation. The man was quickly identified as a brigade member, hauled in and questioned. Royalist interrogation methods were not gentle.

"What's he said so far, Chief?" Jeff glanced at the prisoner, then back to the officer. "I haven't kept Captain Harding up to speed on this."

"Sir, he claims to be only an in-between."

"Go-between, Chief?"

"Exactly Captain Masters. A go-between, a small potato between your Central Intellegency and the enemies of Emir Idris, the holy warrior chosen by Allah and the United Nations to be our most sacred King."

I wanted to ask a dozen questions. Jeff had told me to let him do the talking, so I kept my mouth shut.

"My special officers have extracted such information as this: that this small faction of enemies is backed by the Central Intellegency, Occidental Petroleum's in-country manager and a person within the Egyptian embassy.

Makes sense in CIA and oil-company terms. Cover all bases. Bribe everybody. Take whatever you can get from anybody who will give it.

Jeff sipped tea, said, "You told me last week that the agent Ferrette's name was mentioned. That was volunteered, not supplied?"

The chief looked at the prisoner, at me, at Jeff. "Volunteered?"

"Your people didn't give him the name and he just said yeah to stop the pain?"

"There is no pain, Captain. Not in your sense of the word. The King would not allow it."

And Allah plays golf on the weekends.

"Forgive me, Chief. Ferrette is alleged to have behaved in unreliable and indiscreet ways in the days before his death."

"We did not supply the name, Captain. We knew nothing of this Agent Ferrette."

It's a foursome with Jesus, Mary and Joseph.

"Ask him about a man named Fritsche, Chief."

The police captain picked up a phone and spoke into it.

Beyond the glass, a uniformed soldier entered the interrogation room. His face was masked with a black headscarf, desert-style.

The man strapped to the chair started to scream.

CHAPTER 11

ALL YOU NEED IS LOVE

mbassador Boardman allowed us to stand at attention a full thirty seconds before looking up. When she did, Jeff and I dropped our salutes. She initialed the document she'd been reading and placed it in her out box. "Joe, you told Jackie you had a matter of extreme importance and sensitivity to bring to my attention. Why don't you both take a seat."

Jeff stayed braced. "Madam Ambassador, may I suggest we discuss this matter outside, away from any structure or installations."

"Captain, I can assure you this room is not bugged."

"Ma'am, I don't trust nothing in this country anymore."

"I have a very tight schedule." She glanced at me, not smiling. "My son returns from boarding school tomorrow. I'm clearing my desk so he and I can spend time together."

I took this as a silent warning: *You, Joe, are not going to spend time alone with Cotton. And we are not going to discuss your so-called friendship with him in front of this glorified security guard.*

She wasn't aware that Jeff not only knew of the affair but was as angry about it as she was. He merely knew a different set of damning details. The last thing I'd have done was discuss Cotton's holiday plans in front of Jeff.

She rose and led us out to the garden. The embassy grounds were surrounded by high walls topped with razor wire and shaded here and there by towering date palms. Halting at the edge of the tennis court, Mrs. Boardman threw me a significant look. "I'm having this swept and rolled, Joe. Cotton always says it's not half as good as the Uaddan's courts. But the political situation being what it is locally—"

I wondered which she considered the greater threat to Cotton's safety, Joe Harding or some unknown terrorist.

Jeff surveyed the scene. "This ought to do, ma'am."

"Carry on, then."

"Has the prime minister or anyone else informed you that a local terrorist group intends to attack parliament and attempt to overthrow the government?"

"Are you cleared for this, Captain Masters?"

Jeff's hands turned into fists. "It's my job, ma'am."

Mrs. Boardman looked at me.

"He is cleared, yes, ma'am."

"In general terms, yes, Captain, I am aware of these attempts."

"Specifically a group known as the Islamic Brotherhood Sharia Brigade."

"No, I don't believe that one has come to my attention."

"It's our understanding that the Central Intelligence Agency is supplying them with weapons, specifically British mortars and shells."

The blank expression on the ambassador's face did not change. Her poker-face skills were first rate. "Well, thank you, Captain. I'll have to look into it."

"That attack on the British army camp was a test drive."

"It's your understanding, you say?"

"The Libyan police are already engaged, ma'am. Two men are in custody. And, from what we know, the group has hooked up with a couple of members of parliament, influential men who want the Yanks, King Idris and British Petroleum out of Libya for good. Who'll pay any price."

I cut in. "These opposition people are threatening to talk. BP's in-country manager is also supporting the group. Funding it."

"Trying to play both sides, you mean?"

"To state the obvious, ma'am, just like us."

She looked at Jeff. "You believe this to be a serious, credible threat? To us? To the King's government?"

"These members intend to appeal to the United Nations."

"You can't be serious."

"He is, ma'am. From what we know, your former trade rep, Pete Ferrette, was running this show."

Now her expression did change. She glared at me. "Ah, yes, the indiscreet Mr. Ferrette. To my knowledge, he was involved only with regular transfers of arms to Southeast Asia."

"Looks like some of it was diverted," Jeff said. "Off-loaded here. Code name, Operation Janus. I have witnesses. One of our officers was forced to serve as cover and errand boy. Then, around Christmas, he was killed. To shut him up, we think"

"I wasn't aware of any of that. Might it have been prevented? Terrible, terrible." Her bored, perfunctory tone was the sort most adults reserve for mourning the death of a friend's child's pet cat. "In any case, the Southeast Asia deliveries have stopped. The unit being supplied is no longer operational."

Bingo. Jay, Ted Fritsche, whatever his name is, he claimed to be the lone survivor of a wiped-out unit. And now he's running the show for the local anti-royalist brigade.

"Odds are," I said, "that Ferrette's indiscretions got him killed too. The crash out at Wheelus may have been an accident. We don't think his death was."

Mrs. Boardman turned away for a moment, presumably thinking this through. "Two murders now, in connection with this?" She turned back to face us, fully engaged.

Maybe she can feel something besides love for her boy. "That we know of, ma'am. Two American officers."

"Mr. Ferrette told me he was working on plugging a leak. He called it a diplomatic time bomb. He was scheduled to give me a report the week after he died. He claimed he had to run it by his handlers first. He was going to meet his own case officer in Laos."

"Appears he got his—ah, got caught in the middle," Jeff said.

"Clearly he did, Captain Masters. Does this fit? That he was actually trying to keep me and my superiors at State from any confirmation that the Agency was supporting both the royalists and the insurgents? But he slipped up and said something out of place?"

"Fits like a bulb in a socket."

She looked away. "Darwin."

"Ma'am?"

"Survival of the fittest. Natural selection. Weaker men give in to overwhelming pressure. They are bested by stronger individuals."

Jesus. She can step back from murder like a coroner from a corpse. Diplomats have to be cold, sure. But if I were terminated with prejudice tomorrow, would she feel anything but relief? Would she even share Cotton's pain and sorrow?

"Stating the obvious a second time, ma'am. The Agency ain't no individual."

"Lieutenant Ron Connolly," I said, "the man killed at Christmas, he tried to fight back and protect himself. His sister's a Marine major, works intelligence at the Pentagon. He took leave in November to see her about it. She talked to some higher-ups over there. It looks like she talked to the wrong people, and that it got passed on. Now she's out for blood."

"Who could blame her?" Glancing over my shoulder, she called to a tall man walking toward us—Ted Fritsche, wearing Air Force tans. "I'll be with you in a moment, Major." Turning back to us, she said, "You've given me a great deal to think about, gentlemen. Anything else?"

I figured it might be now or never. "Ma'am, do you happen to know whether that officer over there ever served overseas with Colonel Swanson?"

"You work for the colonel, Joe. Why don't you ask him?"

"Fritsche is Agency, too, isn't he? The uniform's a cover. He doesn't even shine his shoes."

"Joe! Did the lady Marine suggest that?"

"Not exactly, ma'am. But while we're on the subject, and I haven't checked it out personally, a source tells me that Colonel Swanson is wearing military decorations he didn't earn."

That bit of gossip was either going to put me on the road to early promotion or boot me out the door.

"Your source is again the angry lady Marine?"

"An anonymous source, ma'am. You may want to have your people check the Colonel's combat record against what he wears on his chest."

"Captain Harding. This is an extremely serious charge. I want to know right now—"

"I'm sorry, ma'am. I can't say more than that. I'm not charging him with anything. All I can say is that you may want to have it seen to. I could be wrong. I'm speaking to you in what I hope is strict confidence."

I was protecting my sources. Swanson had used my junior clerk as a sexual toilet; Airman Bacon also resented his relationship with the ambassador. My senior clerk, Airman Wilson, an expert in extracting arcane facts from classified files and comparing them to other facts and files, had been shamed and degraded by the colonel. The colonel was getting payback from both. Knowing but not reporting all this was clearly a breach of good order, security and discipline. My incautious remarks could backfire. But if I told the ambassador her boyfriend was two-timing her with enlisted females, and he denied it, who would she believe?

"Very well, gentlemen, our watchwords will be silence and caution, at least for the present. I must confer with my superiors at State."

I glanced at Fritsche.

"At State," she repeated. "State."

Jeff saluted. "We thank you for your time, Madam Ambassador."

"Thank you for your information and counsel, Captain Masters. Ah, by the way. Captain Harding is coming into town for supper on Thursday, a strictly private occasion. Perhaps you would care to join us?"

"Of course, ma'am. Pleasure's all mine."

Captain Motorcycle Boots as chaperone. Nice. This is one tough woman. But she heard me. Her relationship with Swanson is unwise and could blow up in her face. She'll deal with it. My relationship with Cotton is equally dicey. Walter Jenkins, Lyndon Johnson's longtime aide, got caught having sex with another man in a YMCA three blocks from the White House. The scandal hit every front page in America. If she tries to keep me and Cotton separated and we make a fuss, or if Winston Boardman makes a public issue of the Gstaad incident, LBJ will hear about it and her career will be just as cooked as mine.

What are her priorities? Protecting the defunct Laos operation is a minor matter. But she's got to get control of whatever operation Fritsche is running with the locals. And keep the whole thing quiet. She's got to talk to the prime minister. She's going to be busy. It'll all work in my favor.

Our information was solid. Everything we'd said seemed worth the risk.

"Why don't we take some time off," Hal said that afternoon. "See where we are about all this. Do you mind?"

I'd suggested trading rubdowns. My body buddy wasn't interested. This was the first time either of us had said no.

With Cotton due back the next day but presumably unavailable as a lover, and wanting my sex drive under control when I met him on Thursday, I'd stopped by Hal Denman's office that afternoon. Without any preliminaries, I'd suggested getting together after supper.

He'd hesitated, said he had work to catch up on but finally refused outright. "Maybe we've seen too much of each other, Joe. That last time didn't feel so good. I took it as a signal. We got to think about this. It's getting kind of—I don't know."

"Hal, are you saying you never—?"

"No. I'm saying we're friends first, buddies. Right?"

"Absolutely. You're my buddy. Damn right."

"I haven't written Elmo in a month. And it's been twice that long since I heard from him. With you, I'm liking it fine. You talk to me. Doesn't feel right, somehow, though. Know what I mean?"

"Maybe you should take leave and go see him."

"Doesn't work that way. His wife knows about all his—us."

Does she know about Ted Fritsche?

"Sure, I understand. What we've been doing feels real good, except for the last time. I was mentally fucked up. It won't happen again."

I was practically begging.

"Like I say, Joe. Let's take a month off. See where we stand then."

"Sure. A month. You're a champ, Rocky. The best."

Hal Denman had fallen in love with me, and I hadn't even noticed. I'd been too busy earning medals and being a hero; protecting my other sex-buddy, the medic, and mooning over Cotton. Hal himself only noticed when the sex didn't work. Then he had to take stock of what had happened and where each of his affairs was going. That's how I figure it, anyway.

Hal glanced away, as if embarrassed, then looked straight at me. "You're the best, Joe, not me. And I feel like I'm betraying Elmo with you. I still love him. He says he'll divorce her, once the kids are out of school and we retire."

Hal was my buddy, not my lover, and his words put me in a bind.

Rae Connolly had come to distrust McAddams. She believed he'd betrayed her brother and might be dangerous to others. If she was right, Hal's trust was misplaced. But, given the circumstances, I couldn't say so, not until I knew a lot more.

Frustrated and hornier than ever, I jogged four miles, showered at the gym, entered the steam room half an hour before closing and got very, very lucky. One of the two overhead lights was out. Seated at the far, darker end of the room was a young man who was not only eager to play but fun to play with.

Lieutenant Sam Goldman, an F-102 fighter pilot based at Soesterberg Air Base up in the Netherlands and now TDY at Wheelus for training, was a junior edition of Bruce Opstein. Short, solid, moderately muscular, balding, married, whip smart and New York Jewish, he caught and held my stare as I entered the room. He was sitting on his towel. I spread mine out two feet away. By the time I'd settled down, he'd opened his knees a bit and cocked his head. The message was unmistakable: "How about it?"

I touched myself. So did he. This time I had no trouble getting hard. I moved over until our towels were almost touching.

He put his hand on my leg. I let it stay there.

"This OK what I'm doing?" he said.

I nudged his hand higher, then reached for him. "What about this? This OK?'

"You big guys," he whispered, already slightly out of breath. "Takes both hands to do the job."

"Yeah, you're doing great, keep going. What are you, New Jersey? You want me to touch you down in here?"

"No, pull on 'em. Jamaica, Queens. Ha. Man, you're wet already."

"Gonna get wetter. Do that, do that."

"Tighter, yeah. Harder."

"Fuckin' beer can."

"Foam's gonna blow."

We didn't have much time. But the shared quick yank was hot enough to tell me I wanted another session with this guy.

He felt the same. Unlike some men on their own in unfamiliar places, especially ones wearing wedding rings, he didn't simply come and go. We shared a shower, introduced ourselves and traded good-natured jokes about Jack Beanstalk and the horny dwarf. Before we said good-bye, I asked him to meet me at the O club bar for Friday happy hour.

Outside the gym we exchanged salutes. "A Southern man with a nifty plan," he said, throwing me a boyish wink. "The fighter jock will be ready to rock."

Back at the BOQ, satisfied and ready for Thursday, I glanced down the long hall as I unlocked my door. At the far end, a tall man in an aloha shirt and chinos was just entering Hal Denman's suite. I'm sure he didn't see me.

There was now no question about it. Jay the Oilman's shirt belonged to Ted Fritsche. They were the same man, not twins, not look-alikes.

Damn, is this the real reason Hal turned me down? Grown men don't enter other men's quarters this late, not unless they've got something going. Hal's found a new beat-off buddy and he'd already set up this date for tonight.

Wait a minute. There's no way Hal's going to take the kind of abuse and domination Fritsche forced me to accept. He'd kill the bastard first. And Fritsche doesn't strike me as the type of alpha that'll be satisfied with a hand job.

Now I do have to tell Hal that Fritsche's CIA, that he—

Hold on. Rae Connolly said two of Elmo McAddams' younger men are at Wheelus. These must be them. Maybe McAddams' bull boys have to put out for each other, maybe that's part of the deal. Or maybe it's not sex at all. Maybe McAddams gave them some joint project.

Hal's in danger. What do I do?

The private supper with Elizabeth Boardman, Jeff and Cotton was tense but mercifully brief, only three courses. The ambassador tried light conversation but blundered badly when inquiring about Jeff's wife. Jeff was unfamiliar with how to use fish knives and forks. A hunk of mackerel with tomato sauce landed on the starched linen napkin in his lap. Despite the steam-room session with Sam Goldman, my sexual barometer stayed high the whole time. Cotton said practically nothing until, following dessert and coffee, Mrs. Boardman led Jeff into her office for a conference on security matters and left us more or less alone for five minutes.

"I'm going to ride out to the base tomorrow," Cotton whispered.

"No, you're not. Bad idea."

"I'll take a taxi. You can't stop me. Anyway, I need to shop at the BX."

"Fuck the BX. Listen to me."

"I don't want to listen. I want to be. With. You."

"Same here, kiddo. Long term, right? Just us guys?"

He ducked his head. The peace symbol on a chain around his neck clanked against the table. "But if we're never together—?"

"We will be. But for now, we've got to play by her rules."

"I just want to hold you again."

"Same here. But we can't. What about your father?"

"They worked something out. I haven't heard from him. Hope I don't ever. What about Colonel Swanson?"

"A little bird suggested that the relationship is unwise."

Ma'amoud had entered on silent feet. "More coffee, my gentlemens?"

We hadn't heard him. We were talking too much. We said no to refills and he went away.

"Good. I think she's going to let us go to Sabratha. Ma'amoud will drive. We'll take a Marine guard for security."

"A chaperone in camouflage."

"Maybe a week from now."

"I think she's going to let us play tennis."

"Here at the embassy, right. Not at the Uaddan. No naked showers together in the locker room."

"You're busting my nuts, kiddo. I'm not going to be able to stand up when your mama comes back."

"Same here. Hormones, like you said."

"Cool your jets, kiddo. OK? This is going to work out. She has to trust us. Trust this."

"I'll try. I have to."

"Just us guys. Trust *me*, OK?"

Sam Goldman was right on time for our happy-hour date on Friday. In his tailored flight suit, aviator shades and flight boots, he was the hottest man in the room. In my eyes, anyhow.

"How they hanging, Captain?"

"Ready to rock, jet jock."

"Into the air, junior birdman? What are you drinking?"

"Jack and water."

"Later on, we'll cut out the water."

"Got that right."

When he returned with the drinks—two Scotches for him, two JDs for me—I said, "What is it in New York, the cold weather? Better public schools?"

"Cheers. What about New York?"

"Cheers. The way you guys talk. Snappy, coming right back, like jiving only with a different accent. You've even got me doing it."

He settled down in a chair and stared across the table at me, not grinning exactly but pleased. "God-DAMN am I glad I got this assignment. This is choice."

"How long are you here for, Sam?"

"Six weeks, why?"

"Your wife's not coming down?"

"Naah, she'd hate this place. We're cool."

"We?"

"This."

"Right." We clicked glasses again and then drained them.

I should have felt guilty. Maybe Sam should have, too. We were taking a risk, and I was repeating a pattern—fooling around with a younger man who was basically unavailable. But hell, here we were, caught between the desert and the deep blue sea. We were both healthy, horny guys with no better options. Later that night, in bed, we fit together perfectly, without even thinking about it. Sam, like me, had had an older college mentor, a fraternity brother.

"A nice Jewish boy needs a nice Jewish wife," Sam said afterwards, sounding exactly like Ops. "And a horse-cock buddy every so often."

Six weeks, I thought the next morning. *Sam's right. This is choice.*

Only one jarring detail marred an otherwise ideal evening. During happy hour, I spotted Ted Fritsche on the far side of the O club bar. I'd have expected to see Hal Denman at his side. Instead, he entered alone, picked up a pretty nurse within ten minutes and, after two drinks, they left together.

What is this guy? Did Hal turn him down so hard he went straight? Clearly, he leads a very active social life.

My life and Hal's, too, had turned bumpy by Monday afternoon. A few minutes after three, he called to ask if I could meet him in the snack bar for coffee. When I got there, he bought two bottled Pepsis while I found a table away from the crowd. Once seated, he handed me a slip of paper with a Washington DC phone number on it.

"The lady Marine wants to talk to you. Call this number on a secure line. She'll expect the call at sixteen hundred hours our time."

"She didn't say what it's about?"

"I'm only the messenger boy. Speaking of boys, who's the baby-faced pilot I saw you with?"

"He's TDY from Holland. Married. They come and go."

"Look, Joe, I don't want you to think—"

"You said a month, Rocky. I'm fine with that."

"I still haven't heard from Elmo. Guess I shouldn't tell you that."

"He's probably busy. Some project or other."

"Busy" didn't begin to cover it. I called Rae Connolly from the secure phone in the commissary office. She picked up on the first ring and got right to the point.

"Our older friend was interviewed two days ago and again yesterday by your Office of Special Investigations. He'd been fingered by two young Marine lieutenants, locally assigned. They're trying to save their own butts by covering for each other. That's how I got into the case. They're shave-tails right out of Parris Island, still wet behind the ears, dumb as dirt, so they may be OK."

"They claimed he—?"

"Yeah, at the Marine Memorial, half an hour before sunset. It's a known pick-up zone."

"Stupid numb-nuts."

"Got that right. They claim they thought it was just for drinks and a few laughs in his basement. His wife is out of town."

"He's been grilled twice? That serious."

"Right again. He's giving up names himself now."

Oh, shit. Here it comes.

"Any idea—?"

"Only one blue suit so far, a light colonel named Blackwell, last assignment Travis Air Base. An Army lieutenant, home of record, Hilo, Hawaii. A deck ape, submarine service, currently based at Pearl Harbor, home of record, Cincinnati. A Marine lance corporal whose enlistment was up last year."

"He's playing it pretty safe so far. Colonel Blackwell and Lieutenant Naka-mura are dead. Your grunt's back home with his mama. That's one for four."

"You know all the guys on his list?"

"I happen to know about these two. He wasn't mixed up with either one. I'm sure of that."

"Oh, and an agent or case officer with some cover name like Fritz or French."

"We talked about him. You were going to do some digging."

"You cock-sucking bastard. I wondered what you'd say when I mentioned his name."

"He lives in the next building. He works at the embassy."

"Are you part of this, too? He was Army for seven years."

"Sloppy Army. Doesn't know how to shine shoes. That was cover."

"You're wasting my time. When did you rent our friend's basement?"

"I told you. I never met him. He did a favor for a buddy."

Shit. Odds are he'll give up Duane Haynes next. Then Hal. Then me. It may be only a matter of time. They'll grill him until he pees in his shorts—like the sadeek downtown.

"The bastard's met too many of you, that's for sure. Bachelors, fudge-packing perverts, working as a team, using my baby brother who was so straight-arrow he took an instruction manual with him on his honeymoon."

"Believe me, ma'am, I'm on your team, not our friend's or the agent's. Look, he was in a position to help some people. That's how I see it. Got them out of tight situations here. And now he himself is targeted by the witch-hunting zealots."

"I got no sympathy."

"Don't forget, you looked him up on your own. He probably never heard of your brother until then."

"Tell me something I don't know. Christ on a crutch, you must be dumber than bat shit."

"The agent, the fake attaché, he's the key here. Odds are he terminated his handler with extreme prejudice. He took over a local group of revolutionary bandits already set up by the Agency chief he killed. We've warned the ambassador. Best of all, he's got a sexual track record that'll give the asswipes sweating our friend a matching set of five-inch boners. Turn him in now. Or I swear on Caesar's left nut he may turn on you."

"You talk like a DI."

"Thank you, ma'am. Coming from a lady Marine, that's a real compliment."

"Go fuck yourself with a swagger stick. And lose this phone number. I'll think about it."

She's not convinced. How do I warn Duane and save Hal? We may all be royally fucked and I don't have the right weapons. God damn Elmo McAddams. God damn Terry Blackwell. And God damn numb-nuts Ron Connolly—for not saying No and not contacting Jeff.

Captain Hard-on, there must be a graveyard reserved for the men who pass through your life. It could end up full before you even turn thirty.

CHAPTER 12

BOY SCOUTS

The independent Kingdom of Libya was created in 1951 by joining together three colonial territories—Tripolitania, Cyrenaica and the Fezzan—under the auspices and initial control of the United Nations. Emir Idris al-Senussi, an influential guerrilla leader with a considerable religious and political following, was named constitutional monarch. In political terms, this left the nation with three capital cities. In practice, the seat of government was wherever the King and prime minister chose to sleep. Members of council, ambassadors and high officials followed them from place to place in order to conduct business.

On the day I spoke to Rae Connolly, the government had set up shop in Tobruk, a port city to the far northeast, near the Egyptian border. Ambassador Boardman was ordered there by Washington on Tuesday, taking with her two secretaries, a translator, Marine guards, her son Cotton, her butler Ma'amoud, the attaché Major Fritsche, and Colonel Swanson. Before they left, it was agreed that Cotton and I would be allowed to tour the Roman ruins at Sabratha the following Saturday. Ma'amoud and a guard would accompany us on the day-long excursion. Tennis and lunch at the embassy were set for Sunday. These arrangements gave me reason to hope that the tight restrictions on our friendship would gradually be loosened. Work-wise, the week was routine. With Colonel Opstein pushing my pared-down agenda, the weekly staff meeting finished in under an hour. Airplanes taking off from Wheelus scored the same number of landings. A surveillance team set up by Jeff and Sergeant Ward collared an elderly but seemingly pregnant local lady who enjoyed base-exchange privileges. Frisked by a matron, she turned out to be shoplifting a ten-pound canned ham. A drunken sergeant driving an Austin hit a donkey cart on the Mellaha highway and ran his car off the road. The sergeant was taken first to base hospital, then to jail. The unfortunate donkey had to be destroyed, its value to be deducted from the sergeant's paychecks and paid to the owner.

And I received a wire datelined Falls Church, Virginia:

REPORT FILED STOP AWAITING OUTCOME STOP
SIT TIGHT. STOP ANGEL.

Sam Goldman and I got together twice more, once in his bed, once in mine, with excellent results both times. The demands we made on each other were reasonable and few, the results surprisingly pleasant. Like Hal and Duane, this sexy, loving man would be difficult to give up.

I didn't run into Hal until Thursday. We were both headed to the gym so we changed together and I spotted him while he lifted weights.

"Something's going on, Joe." Although I was staring at his face upside down, the worried expression was easy to read. "I called Elmo's office. The girl that answered said he'd taken a short leave of absence."

Uh-oh. Sounds worse than just a couple of interviews.

"I thought about calling his house."

"I wouldn't do that."

"No."

"Maybe Ted Fritsche knows something about it," I said.

"Who?"

"I saw him go into your room, late one night."

Hal set the weights aside and turned to face me. "No, you didn't."

"He's one of Elmo's boys, right?"

"Forget what you saw. It doesn't mean anything."

"I don't own you. It's none of my business what you do. But you're right. Something's up, something big. And you'd better put distance between you and him. Fast."

"You heard something from Major Connolly? What did she tell you?"

"What I just said. The less you know the better. Deny everything. Admit nothing. Name, rank and serial number. For right now, steer clear of Fritsche. He's radioactive. Unless I miss my guess, he's in big trouble, or about to be."

"She's certain? You are?"

"Trust me, Hal. She said to sit tight. And that's what I'm doing."

Have you ever noticed that when a supervisor wishes to correct a subordinate, or suggest a course of action that the subordinate is sure to dislike, he or she often conducts the interview away from the office? I'd done it myself weeks before, with Airman Bacon.

Colonel Swanson returned on Friday morning and, in an unusual move, asked me to lunch with him at Il Gattopardo, his favorite off-base hangout, a grim Italian café near his villa. The décor was masculine and local: stuffed antelope heads, antique rifles, brass trays, handmade rugs and a large, framed photograph of King Idris. The food matched the setting: spaghetti topped with acidic red sauce, overcooked veal cutlets, rolls just this side of stale, Italian beer that tasted months past the sell-by date.

Lunch wasn't the point, of course. The pro forma reason for the meeting was to bring me up to speed on the Conroy-Totenberg fiasco.

"Joe," the colonel began, "you and Ops and his team did a helluva fine job handling that series of royal screw ups. I wanted to let you know that Major Larsen, the exec of the 155th, commended you personally for helping him wrap up his reports. It'll come down on paper and will go in your file."

I'd helped as little as possible. To tell everything I knew would have cost me my career. "That's good to hear, sir."

"Which is right in line with the outstanding qualities you display as an administrator. Stay on the ball, son, and you'll go a long way."

This isn't sounding good. Don't lose your cool. Listen to every word he says. "Thank you, sir. I try to do my best."

A waiter with dirty hands set down bowls of pasta. The colonel kept silent until the man withdrew.

"What they came up with, Joe, to satisfy the families and goddamn reporters and all, was to blame it on Republic Aviation. Said the maintenance manual for the D model F-105 contained a chart pertaining to the afterburner that was faulty or incomplete—something like that. The error has been corrected. Republic went down the tubes anyway. Bought up by Fairchild."

"So they didn't have to blame—?"

"Exactly. The Department of the Air Force can plausibly claim that, in both cases, the afterburners went haywire. The pilots weren't at fault. The ugly rumors and all that—a bunch of baloney."

Plausible deniability, the tool of so many successful leaders. "That's also good to hear, sir. A comfort to their wives and families."

"Wanted to let you know, too, that your old commander was permanently committed to a private asylum in South Carolina last month. The state and the Veterans Administration have joint custody. Poor guy. His wife fought it, of course."

I wasn't going to touch that one, either. "A great lady, a tragedy for her."

"Drinks, does she?"

"Commander's lady, it's not the easiest job in the world."

"My ex-wife—well, never mind that."

For a moment, I thought he was going to get personal. Instead, he tucked a napkin under his chin, dug into the pasta and said, "Another reason I wanted to talk to you, Joe, there's just one little problem I'd like you to think about. A misstep, I might say, surprising in an officer of your abilities."

Here it comes. "Sir?"

"It has been brought to my attention, son, that you've been opening your mouth too much in public."

"I see, sir." I didn't, but several possibilities came to mind.

"Specifically the alleged attack on the Brits by alleged anti-revolutionary forces."

A forkful of spaghetti gave me time to think. "In public, sir?"

"An embassy reception is a public affair, Joe."

The British captain of intelligence already dressed me down for this. He'd then tattled to daddy. It was easy to guess why.

"Sir, I did mention it to one of the Brit spies. The attack is pretty fully covered in our briefing books."

"Which are top secret, Captain. In short, and to finish this up, your job description does not include discussing sensitive diplomatic and military matters without authorization. The conversation with Captain Marchmain was way out of line. You are known to have powerful friends and excellent connections. Don't get above yourself."

Careful, Joe. "Sir, I certainly understand. I'm glad you brought this up. I'll definitely watch my words in the future."

"Enough said, then. This sauce is pretty good, huh? And it looks like Airman Buster Wilson's lost a couple of pounds. He getting some exercise? Good job, Joe."

Jeff Masters and I hit happy hour that night, stayed for steak dinners with a bunch of junior officers and drank brandy in the bar for at least another hour. Sometime after midnight, Ted Fritsche used a passkey to unlock the door to my BOQ bedroom. Once inside, he shined a flashlight in my eyes and ordered me to dress.

I wasn't thinking straight. I was still half drunk. He outranked me. I followed orders.

Minutes later he used the passkey to enter Hal Denman's suite.

"On your feet, One-Punch. Get out of them skivvies. Strip. You, too, Hard-on. Down to your skin."

"What the hell, Ted?"

"Get 'em off, Champ. You two boys are going to give each other rubdowns. I'm gonna watch."

Hal's face turned white. One on one, he knew his way around a bedroom or an Oriental carpet. But I doubt that he ever dreamed of putting on a sex show. Instead of shucking off his shorts, he positioned his hands modestly in front of his crotch.

"No way, Ted. That's filthy dirty. I wouldn't ever. You're drunk or doped up. Go someplace else to get your jollies."

Fearful and still half-asleep but hoping to compromise Fritsche with a witness, I stupidly followed instructions. Stripping down, I pulled on my dick seductively and took Hal by the hand. "We're going to fix the problem," I whispered. "Forget he's here. Pretend the month is up. I want you now. Let me get these off you. OK? Trust me, Rocky."

Once I got Hal on his back on the handmade rug, he began to cooperate, though with no real passion. Kneeling between his legs, I stroked him the way I knew he liked. Shaking, he reached up and wrapped his hands around my ears.

Fritsche, standing above and behind Hal's head, dropped a hand to his own crotch, unzipped his pants, and started talking. His voice was low, his tone definitely threatening but also, under the circumstances, voluptuous. "You two timeservers are meddling in matters far too important to be put at risk for nothing. United States foreign policy is at stake. You've wandered into a situation you know nothing about. You're way, way off the reservation, and it could get dangerous— for you, for your slightly stupid buddy, the muscle-bound cop, and for a lot of other people."

Hal's hands had moved to my tits, pinching them lightly. His dick had grown solid in my hand. Aroused but starting to panic, I tried to touch Fritsche's leg, stupidly imagining I could pull him down beside us.

He slapped my hand away. "I changed my mind. This is good. You boys are going to fuck each other. And I'm gonna watch that. I've had you both and you're a pair of worthless screws. Couldn't sell either one of your sorry asses for a nickel in a Bangkok bar." Grinning, he pulled out his hardening cock. "But I figure maybe if we rub you two boy scouts together, and then you start plugging holes ..."

"Fuck you, Mister." Hal was suddenly on his feet, fists clenched, looking inches taller than his full five-nine.

"No, fuck him," Fritsche replied. "You go first. You're the senior officer. He needs fucking. He fucks boys, one underage boy in particular, or so they say downtown. Real pervert. Prove you ain't, Hal, my pal. Fuck him hard."

He either didn't know or, in his aroused state, had forgotten the details of Denman's prize-fighting career. Old One-Punch went ballistic. Fritsche was on the floor in two seconds.

"You sorry piece of shit," Hal whispered, aware of the BOQ's thin walls. "You were on the ropes until Elmo ordered me to reel you in—after your worthless buddies got overrun by a bunch of gooks. Sobbing and crying about you'd lost your whole network, lost your handler, man you loved, only man on God's green earth you'd do anything for. I gave you a shoulder to cry on, I didn't give you anything else."

It all fit together. Suddenly sober again, I was on my feet beside Hal. "That was Cheeto, the Bird and Zulu? He cried on my shoulder, too. Sounds like his whole agency string died in a wipe-out. I listened to him bawl. And that's why he's back in Tripoli. Trying to recoup what's left of the local operation."

Hal nodded once. "Comes down to it, Ted or whatever your name is, you made an improper suggestion, a proposal, at that time. I knew you were hurting, not in control of yourself, your emotions all bent out of shape. So I didn't turn you in. Did you a favor, know what I mean?"

"Fuck you, One-Punch."

"That was a real mistake on my part, Ted. I've made plenty in my time. But that's numero uno on the list. I should have kicked your rotten asshole all the way up to your teeth, Elmo or no Elmo. And I should have reported you then. Had your sorry ass thrown in jail."

I'd never seen this side of Hal. He'd won Golden Gloves and been a top military prize-fighter. His muscular bravery, the armor of a warrior, was real. This was no pallid, deferential ex-navigator wielding a slide rule. Here was a man I could fight beside. Hal and I were now a team, deadly and invincible as the Greek warrior-lovers Cotton and I only pretended to be.

"Yes, sir, Major Denman," I said. "This officer, whoever he is, asked me to do dirty things with him, too, at the Uaddan Hotel. Tried to pick me up in the casino bar. Made immoral, unnatural suggestions. You think I should turn him in for that? There were witnesses. Or maybe we both should do it, right now. That would stick."

"I wouldn't rule it out, Captain."

Fritsche, six inches taller than Denman, and just as wide, tried to get Denman by the knees. Denman put him down again. "This is getting boring, Fritsche. You know? If you want to make threats, you'd better learn how to listen." He looked up at me. When I nodded, he continued, his tone harder, deeper and more muscular—the voice Rocky Marciano must have used on opponents when stepping into the ring.

"The death of a man based here was not only suspicious but covered up. And you're telling us that's above our pay grades?" Hal gave Fritsche a shove. "Fuck off, Major. Get out of my quarters. Forget we exist. Move."

"The colonel—"

I picked it right up. "Another man was murdered when that C-130 bought the farm. We think we know who did it."

"You can't prove—"

"One more word," I continued, "and we're going to the OSI and file charges tonight. How's this? You forced your way into our private quarters. You exposed yourself to us, made improper and illegal suggestions and advances, attempted to persuade us to commit sodomy and to betray our oaths to uphold the law, the Constitution, the Uniform Code of Military Justice, Air Force regs and the security and good order of the United States Air Force."

When my blood is up, I can sure pile it on. But any officer worth his salt should be able to do the same. Even stark naked.

Fritsche threw Denman the ice-blue stare that had conquered me and, presumably, Denman himself. It didn't work this time. "Unlock the door, Joe," Hal said. "This individual is leaving."

Fritsche hauled to his feet. "You boy scouts don't know what you've got yourselves into. You're dog meat. Road kill. Grease on the tarmac."

Once he was gone, Denman locked the door, crossed himself, closed his eyes and took me in his arms. "I run Personnel, Joe. I ride herd on a bunch of clerks. What the heck is happening? Our careers are over, you think?"

"I think your buddy at the Pentagon dealt us marked cards from a stacked deck. He had a lot more to do with this than he said. And now his two-timing ass is up the creek. It's us against them. You with me?"

"Could turn in my papers tomorrow, be out of here in a month." Hal kissed my neck, ran his fingertips up and down my backbone, kissed me again. "What do you mean, 'up the creek'?"

"Hold it. You're not cleared. Let me think."

"You want me to risk my career turning in Elmo and Ted but not know why? What the heck's happened to Elmo?"

Hal was right. In military intelligence terms, he had a need to know. "The OSI's got your daddy by the balls and he's naming names, trying to save his own lying skin. Fritsche is CIA or the next thing to it. Remember Ferrette, the embassy trade rep, so called? Died when the C-130 ate the bakery? Trade rep was his cover. From what I can tell, he talked too much. Fritsche killed him, then replaced him. Fritsche's probably not his name. The one time we did get together he was wearing that blue and orange Hawaiian shirt he wore when he visited you. Said his name was Jay and claimed to work in the oil fields."

"That's when he broke down about Cheeto and the Zulu and—?"

"Check. He's since switched wedding rings. He must have forgotten to lose the shirt. CIA's playing both ends against the middle with the Libyans. My guess is that Colonel Swanson's involved in this right up to his wheel cap. With another very serious problem yet to answer for."

Hal crossed himself again. His face had gone from pink to red to near-white again. "Jesus, Mary and Joseph. Dirty, all of them. You're right, sure. We've got to stop him. Take him out. Before one of them does something—I don't know, worse? Fingers us, in a way we can't stop?" He shook his head. "It can't be true about Elmo, just can't."

I was drained. The last thing I wanted to think about was tomorrow, or Elmo, or what Fritsche might do, who he might tell, who'd back him—and how we'd have to watch our backs and every word we said.

Standing on his toes, Rocky managed to lick my right ear, then my mouth. "You've got whiskey on your breath, Joe. Probably it's not the greatest idea to swear out a complaint when you're drunk."

"I'm sober enough to fuck you. Or whatever you want me to do."

Hal touched my side. "Tomorrow? First thing? We go to Captain Masters?" And then he fell in against me and whispered, "Rats. Second thing. I've pulled duty tomorrow. Officer of the day. Supposed to report in at o-eight-hundred. I'll have to get out of it."

"Find a substitute. Your lovely administrative assistant, Lieutenant What's-her-name? Twist her tit."

"Lieutenant Zaring, yeah, she owes me a day."

We were skin to skin from ears to cocks. "You think of everything, Joe. If you'd been my manager, I'd have quit the service and turned pro. Been a world cham-peen."

"You're my champ, Rocky. All the way."

"We got to set our clocks for real early, like six. And get some shut-eye."

"Six, yeah, Rocky."

"But do you think maybe now, right now, we could finish what we started, something like that?"

Marciano had slowly dissolved into a cautious, needy boy. I knew we should dress, drag Jeff out of bed, call the embassy, take steps. But I was too drained to act, too worried to do anything but give in to Hal's touch, his crushing disappointment and desperate desire. I couldn't refuse him. I couldn't say no.

"Yeah, Hal. Something like that. We got to forget Fritsche wanting to watch us."

"You can fuck me, if you really want to. It's OK now. Just go slow."

"Rocky?"

"That pervert. A peeping Tom. You like it when I do this?"

"Yeah, the fucker. A real pervert. He got excited when we started mixing it up. He liked what he saw as much as doing it. Yeah, Rocky, do that. Yeah, oh fuck. Keep doing that."

I rousted Jeff out of bed at o-seven-hundred. After picking up coffee and do-nuts, we arrived at Colonel Opstein's villa a few minutes past eight. Ops opened the door wearing a T-shirt and gym shorts. He was carrying a pistol. After he let us inside, he locked the weapon in a drawer in his den.

"In here, guys. My wife's still asleep." He shut the door behind us. "What's up?"

"Trouble," I said. "You remember how I pulled strings to get the flight surgeon and doper clerk reassigned to Nam and out of our air space?"

"Only too well. And your buddy, the medic. Is he OK?"

"As far as I know, sir. But he could be in danger."

"How so?"

"The man I contacted, that made the transfers, a colonel at that time, now a brigadier, Major Denman used to fly with him."

"I never knew the details. No need to know."

"The OSI's got his dick in the wringer and he's naming names."

"And you boys both know how polite that bunch can be?"

"Bastards," Jeff half-growled, half-whispered.

"And you're afraid you and Hal Denman could be a couple more of this man's burnt offerings?"

"For starters."

"Son, I didn't sign that commendation letter just to see some washed-up administrator in Washington ruin your career. And Hal, with his record in the ring? No way. You men are both too valuable to the service."

"Thank you, sir, but—"

"I can look into it first thing Monday, vouch for you two. I got a few strings to pull myself. And Colonel Swanson, I know he speaks highly of you, too."

"Sir, it's worse than that."

Jeff punched his open left hand with his fist. "The colonel, he ain't gonna be no help, looks like. He's got his own problems."

"One at a time, guys. The colonel?"

"The colonel is wearing a Vietnam Service ribbon, Sir."

My clerks had done the research. Jeff now opted to take the fall in case this blew up in our faces. As far as the Elmo McAddams affair went, he was not involved.

"After a thorough search of available records, it appears that the closest the colonel's been to Nam is Anderson Air Base, Guam."

"You've got to be kidding. Have you asked him about it?"

"Sir?"

"No, of course you couldn't do that. Who else knows?"

"Madame Ambassador Boardman."

"Who told her?"

"I did," I said. "She's been seen around town with him, table-for-two kind of thing. She and her son are friends of mine. If the colonel takes a hit, it could spill over onto her. She's having it checked out, too."

"He could face charges."

"Worst case," Jeff said. "Air Force cuts his buttons off."

"They don't do that anymore. Not our concern then. What else?"

I picked up the story. "According to available records, Major Fritsche, the attaché, was also at Anderson."

"So?"

"That's probably not his name. He's probably not even Air Force. First time I met him, he called himself Jay and claimed to work for an oil company."

"You boys are better than the *Herald Tribune*. Except you're handing me speculation and hearsay evidence, not facts."

Somebody knocked on the door. Startled, I jumped. I had worse news to report. "Come."

Mrs. Opstein looked in. "Hello, boys. I'm making coffee. Anybody for eggs and toast and orange juice?"

"Yes all around, dear. Call us when you're ready."

The door closed.

"He's CIA or something like it. Started out in the army. He's running the revolutionary group that attacked the Brits out at Idris Airport. Odds are he's behind whoever killed Lieutenant Connolly last Christmas. He was aboard the C-130 that crashed into the bakery and killed six men. I'm pretty sure he killed his predecessor at the embassy, Pete Ferrette, and got both murders covered up. My guess is that he reports direct to Colonel Swanson."

"Give me one fact I can use, Joe."

"The revolutionary group downtown has a name. That's courtesy of the Marine Corps' intelligence shop at the Pentagon. The local police have at least two members in custody."

"Holy baloney."

"Same source says Fritsche was part of an operation in Laos that got wiped out, all except him."

"Easy enough fact to check."

"The ambassador is aware of most of this," Jeff added.

"You boys working for her or for me?" Ops was already operating on the assumption that he'd soon regain the title "acting wing commander."

"Both, sir," I said.

"Does that wrap it up?"

"Three more facts, sir."

"Shoot."

The door opened. "Coffee and juice are on the table, boys."

"Right there, hon. Keep talking, Joe."

"Fritsche or whatever his real name turns out to be is mixed up with Elmo McAddams, the brigadier getting his teeth pulled back in D.C. Two, he's aware that his cover's blown. Last night he threatened me and Major Denman with bodily harm and a lot worse if we didn't give up and keep quiet. He's some kind of pervert. You don't want to know the details. We're both prepared to swear out complaints against him."

"Let's see where this goes first."

"Three, my source at the Pentagon has reported him to the OSI."

"The charge being—?"

"Don't know, sir. Impersonating an officer would be good enough to hold him for questioning."

"We need to liaise with the ambassador. Let's eat fast and hustle our butts over to my office. That phone is secure. Then I can consider my options."

On the way back to base I explained that the ambassador's son and I were scheduled to go on a day trip to the Sabratha ruins.

"It ought to be safe, Sir. We're taking a Marine guard and the ambassador's butler. Ma'amoud doubles as Cotton's bodyguard."

"I don't know, Joe."

"It's been planned since Easter." This was a stretch but I didn't want to spend the weekend tracking Fritsche. "The ambassador's secretary reconfirmed the whole thing. We'll be out of the way."

"OK, tentatively approved, depending. But don't take this car. Anybody can see it's a personal vehicle. If there's trouble, you'd be sitting ducks. If you do go, take a staff car with an armed driver. And file your complaint with the OSI first."

Once inside Ops' office, I phoned Jackie, the ambassador's private secretary, on the secure line. She could best coordinate the change of plans and vehicles. I was due at the embassy in less than an hour. The phone might as well have exploded in my face.

"Captain Harding, where are you? What's the matter?"

"I'm still at Wheelus. I'm getting a staff car and driver. We—"

"No, you can't be," Jackie half shouted. "Captain, you and the staff car picked up Cotton and Ma'amoud thirty minutes ago."

"What? No, no—"

"There was a message saying you'd be early. That you'd been assigned an air policeman and the Marine could take a day off. You called the guard post."

"You mean he's gone?"

"You're not with him?"

I concentrated on Ops's desktop, the blotter-size calendar, hand carved pen holder, Thai-style name plate and matching in and out boxes. I was trying not to panic, hoping this was all a big mistake, willing Cotton to be safe in his room at the embassy and not in the hands of who knew what kind of bandits.

"No, I told you. Hold on just a—"

Ops slapped my back gently, took the phone out of my hand and politely demanded that Jackie connect him to the Marine guards' detachment commander. The ambassador came on first. Ops explained what appeared to have happened in a couple of short sentences.

"No, ma'am. Of course not. ... No, I was aware of those plans. ... Yes, I know you do. ... No, definitely not. Joe hasn't been out of my sight in the last three hours."

We're completely fucked if it crossed her mind that I'd abduct Cotton. Maybe he mentioned running away together to be hippies? Maybe she saw the clippings he showed me last Easter? He's a man now but he's still got a boy's dreams. Damn, but I love my impetuous junior Beanstalk. God, don't let him get hurt.

I wasn't facing facts. Cotton might already be dead. A ransom note would be delivered. Or a body part. I suddenly felt drunk again, nauseous, dizzy. My heart was beating double time. I had to take deep breaths and stare at the floor to keep from rushing downtown and starting the search myself.

"Potentially an international incident. Yes, ma'am, I understand that. A grave crisis. ... Good. Yes, I know it's Saturday. ... Oh, OK, your people can contact the prime minister's office anyway. ... Jeff, Captain Masters . ... Oh, you do? He'll call his contact, local police chief, put an APB on the car. ... All Points Bulletin, ma'am. No, no, let's not even think that way. We'll find him. ... Now if you would put your Marine commander on the line. He and Jeff will have to coordinate this rescue plan."

Rescue. APB. Let's not even think that way.

I'm already thinking that way. I may never see him again. I've hardly gotten to know him and he may be gone. I want my boy back.

Jeff knows about me and Cotton. How the hell do we play this?

Buddies back each other in a crisis. It's OK.

I was damned if I'd fall apart in front of Ops and Jeff. We had work to do. Jeff phoned the guard shack and instructed his desk sergeant to detail a search party for Major Denman, who should have caught up with us by now, and had not. I picked up another phone and asked the base operator to locate Jeff's new toilet mate, the motor pool officer. A second search had to start there.

CHAPTER 13

AIR POWER

The phone on Ops's desk rang about an hour later. It was Hal, patched through from the base switchboard, asking for me. Ops hit a button, activating the speaker phone.

"They've got us. We don't know who they are except Ted. Locals wearing scarves grabbed me when I exited the BOQ. Chloroform, maybe. Don't know where we—ow! OK, I'll tell him."

"We? Jesus, Hal. Is the boy with you?"

"He wants me to—what he wanted us to do. Ordered me to."

Fritsche wanted to watch Hal fuck Cotton. He'd picked the wrong stud. Hal Denman had never fucked anything livelier than a pillow.

Bile churned from my gut up to my throat. I'd essentially raped Cotton in Gstaad. If Hal couldn't perform, Fritsche might take over. If he abused the boy as he had me, Cotton would either bleed to death or never trust another man again.

Shit. Hal and I should have alerted Jeff and Ops the minute Fritsche left Hal's BOQ. Instead, we got all lovey-dovey and followed it up with nice little naps. Balls for brains.

Fool. You let the bastard get away. You may have killed Cotton and Hal by giving in to the easy thing. We've got to find them, fast.

"And then he'll let us go."

"Do that to Cotton? You can't—"

"Or he'll kill us. Doesn't matter, he says. Elmo used you and me, played us like fish, did favors so we'd go along when he and Ted needed us later. Ted says, anyhow—all of us. We're dog meat, Elmo included. Ted swears he's already—ow! I'll tell him."

"Tell me what? What, Hal?"

"If she wants her boy back, Mrs. Boardman admits she signed off on divert-ing arms to the locals. The local group killed Connolly as a thank-you card. She approved the attack on the Brits' camp. She agreed to let you do her son if you'd keep quiet about it."

What the hell has turned One Punch Denman into a whimpering hostage? Six hours ago he put Fritsche on the floor. Twice.

And then I heard a shout, a scream edged with terror, Cotton's voice, hurting and fearful: "No! Please."

At least he's still alive. Both of them are.

Suddenly Fritsche was on the line. "One more thing, Captain Limpdick. What I need is, we sort all this out and call a truce. I get a guarantee of safe passage to the flight line. Once I'm in the air, you get your boyfriends back."

And then a low, bellowing cry, Cotton again. He and Hal were being tortured or, at least, coerced.

"Major, there's no way to—"

"We'll call back in two hours for the right answer from the madam A. I'm gonna have me some fucky-fucky show while I wait."

And then the phone went dead. Fritsche's get-out-of-jail-free cards—Cotton and Hal—trumped mine.

"Safe passage," I whispered. And then it hit me. Planes and crews equipped to collect bodies, bury evidence and buy silence had arrived at Wheelus within twenty-four hours of the deaths of Ferrette and Connolly. I was on my feet. "Sir, you'd better call the tower."

"For what, son?" Ops was decent enough to ignore the boyfriends issue. And the vicious remark about fucking Cotton.

I quickly outlined my hunch.

Ops had Thornell Riddle, the flight controller, on the line in twenty seconds. He asked a question, scowled, asked another. "Inbound from where? ETA?"

Riddle talked some more and Ops pumped his fist up and down. "Divert him back to Torrejon. Wheelus and Idris are both socked in. Gale-force winds driving a sand storm from the Sahara. What? Well, they are if I say so. Do we have planes in the air? Divert to Malta or Benghazi. Post all fire trucks and tugs down the middle of both runways. Call your buddies at Idris International. Tell 'em anything, a plot to kidnap the King and Crown Prince, that should work. Shut down operations at least until dawn. Keep me posted. Good man."

Ops came around the desk and slapped me on the back. "KC-135 inbound from McGuire, New Jersey. Unscheduled. Torrejon controller just passed him on to us. Good man, Joe. Quick thinking, as usual."

Jeff reentered the room, saluted Ops and opened a small notebook. "He took Colonel Swanson's personal staff car."

"And his regular driver?"

"No, sir. A new driver, recently arrived in fact."

Ops ran his hands across his shaved dome. "No surprise there, son. What about your toilet mate, the motor pool officer?"

"He slept in, sir. So did his top sergeant."

"I'll deal with him next week."

"Far as we can tell, it's the only Chevrolet staff car signed out off base. I'm betting somebody's spotted it."

"You've alerted your friends downtown?"

"The chief, he said his boys had just brought in another candidate for questioning. Said he thought he might ask about where you can hide a blue Chevrolet sedan with a spit shine and Air Force plates and not be noticed."

"That's a long shot, son."

"The chief's troops are working the streets. He's liaising with the ambassador's Marine guys. My best sharpshooter, Sergeant Ward, is outside, ready to take out some bandits."

"Count me in," I said. Jeff and Ward had seen me shoot. They knew I could handle a pistol.

"Way ahead of you, Joe. Ward's got you a weapon and ammo, helmet, armored vest—everything but the G.I. Joe nameplate. Got my patrol car gassed up outside."

Ops opened a drawer and pulled out a revolver and shoulder holster. "Let's get moving, guys."

Ops explained Fritsche's demands to the already frantic ambassador in her private office. Hardly a weak or indecisive woman to begin with, his account turned her into a tigress protecting a newborn cub.

"Torturing my boy? Sexually? An American case officer is involved in this? If Cotton's been touched in any way I'll shuck the pervert's oysters with my bare hands. I'll serve them on toast points to his masters at Langley. I don't care if he's Lyndon Johnson's brother-in-law."

A Libyan wearing elaborate robes and head scarf entered the room, salaamed and handed her a card.

Her manner and tone immediately shifted to diplomatic mode. "Thank you, Doctor. Kindly inform the prime minister I appreciate his efforts to personally bring this situation to a satisfactory conclusion. The Secretary of State knows well his wisdom and generosity." Bowing again, the man backed out of the room.

Mrs. Boardman threw looks at her Marine-guards major and Ops. "Safe passage, gentleman? I don't know where to begin. The Africa desk at State has tried to contact their CIA counterparts. Also NIS. But it's the middle of the night over there. No one is willing to comment or intervene without permission from above. The Secretary was at a fund-raiser for Senator Smathers in Palm Beach."

Ops held up a hand. "I open the airports back up, we let his rescuers take him, we tail the suckers with a posse of F-105s. Once we get our boys back, we blow the plane out of the sky. Piece of cake."

"Colonel, do you really think Washington would approve shooting down one of our own airplanes?"

"We can't trust these people, ma'am. No, we have to find where they are, now. And take them out."

"You could throw him a bone, ma'am," I said. "Prepare a signed statement that you approved the arms diversion and attack on the Brits. Give it to a neutral party, maybe the Swiss ambassador. He trades the statement for physical possession of your boy and Major Denman, alive and well. Then he gets his safe passage."

"And *then* gets a set of rockets up his tailpipes," Jeff said. "Doesn't matter who's driving the plane. They're all bad guys."

Mrs. Boardman glared at me, ignoring Jeff. "I won't even dignify this man's mention of a deviant relationship between you and my son, Captain. I don't know who could have suggested such a thing. Do you?"

I could think of half a dozen including Jeff, Winston Boardman, the locker room attendants at the Uaddan and various members of the ambassador's staff. After all, Fritsche nominally worked at the embassy and spent time at the casino. My guess was a whispered word from Ma'amoud, perhaps traded for money or other favors. The servant had already betrayed the ambassador's affair with Colonel Swanson to her son.

I said what she wanted me to say, with witnesses. "We're friends, ma'am. We play tennis and word games and we swim laps. You and the colonel and Captain Masters all know that. People with dirty minds say dirty things."

"What do you know of Major Fritsche, Captain?"

"That that's probably not his real name or title, as we told you. To my knowledge, he's what you say, a deviant, a pervert, a loose grenade with poisoned testosterone."

"To your—?"

"He demanded that Major Denman and I do things to each other, very specific criminal acts. He wanted to both watch and participate. We of course refused."

"And you didn't turn him in?"

"This happened overnight, ma'am. Sometime after midnight. I went to Captain Masters to file a complaint at o-seven-hundred hours."

Jeff nodded agreement. "About this and all the rest of it, ma'am. It was time to reel him in. We missed capture by maybe an hour."

"And so this is his payback. He takes Joe's young friend and Joe's upright buddy as hostages and—"

The phone beside the ambassador's hand rang. She identified herself and made notes on a pad but said little during a call that lasted perhaps three minutes. Finally, she said "Thank you, Mister Secretary," and put the phone down.

Covering her eyes with her hands, it was clear she hadn't at all liked what she'd heard. "Why did I let my baby boy come back to this place?" And then, to us, "Langley disclaims all responsibility. Their area principal told the Africa desk that he's a contract worker, not really Agency at all. And you're right, gentlemen. Major Ted Fritsche is his cover. His name is Harris. Or at least it is as far as they are willing to say."

The Marine major leaned forward. "Sounds like they don't want him back."

"Apparently not. The secretary is extremely unhappy about this attempt to assist an anti-royalist splinter group. And that it was run out of this building. President Johnson's policy is very clear. We support the legitimate government of the Kingdom of Libya."

"What does the secretary suggest, ma'am?"

"Your Marine guards and Captain Masters' men will act in concert with the royal police or royal army as designated by the local authorities. Move as swiftly as possible, given the circumstances. The primary concern is the safe return of my son and Major Denman."

"And Mister Harris, ma'am?"

"While it is desirable that he be questioned and given a fair trial, his safety is a secondary or even tertiary concern."

He's a dead man. Fine with me.

She shook her head. "What were they thinking, not informing me?"

"Any mention of the KC-135 I ordered back to Spain, Ma'am?"

"No. Langley may not know about the diversion yet. Certainly they would disclaim any connection between such a mission and their operative."

The phone rang again. The ambassador answered but almost immediately handed the receiver to Jeff.

"Good, Chief," Jeff said. "Excellent. We're saddled up and ready to go."

He put down the phone. "Police lieutenant's on the way over. We go from here."

Mrs. Boardman got to her feet. "They've found him? Them?"

"The chief thinks so. A canary in the rebel group chirped, named a couple of brigade members, including the owner of a garage in the Arab souk. Cops on the street asked around. Word came in a few minutes ago. A blue Chevy sedan was seen near there earlier this morning."

Mrs. Boardman waved her hand as if flicking off a mosquito. "Captain Masters, order your guards to locate Colonel Swanson and escort him here."

"Ma'am?"

"He'll need to be questioned about his relationship with Mr. Harris."

"Anderson Air Base, Guam," I said without thinking. "Previous assignments for both, at least on paper."

"Joe, you have a mind like a steel trap—you forget nothing."

"Voltaire, ma'am. I hope I learn from my mistakes. Unlike the French kings."

"Specifically the Bourbons."

"Exactly ma'am."

She even trades quotations like Cotton. That's where he got it.

Her attention returned to Jeff. "Make no mistake. It must be made clear to your men—and to the Colonel. He has no options. He is my subordinate in this country. He will report directly to me."

Jeff reached for the secure phone on his side of the desk.

"The Mediterranean desk at State," Mrs. Boardman, added, "will contact US-AFE and the Defense Department once we know where we are on all this. Make the call, Captain."

Jeff called his guard shack and issued orders.

Ops looked at his watch. "We got less than an hour."

A royal police lieutenant entered the office, saluted and identified himself. "My men is surrounded the area, Madame Ambassador. You may depend, Your Excellency, that we do everything in our power for the safe return hereof. If I may—?" He unrolled a map and spread it across the desk. It was a detailed chart of every building of every block of the souk. Pointing, he said, "Just here."

An L-shaped compound identified in Arabic lettering lay beneath his finger.

Jeff leaned in closer, ran his own finger down one street, then another, looked at me and whispered, "Well I'll be damned."

We'd walked past the garage a dozen times. We always parked one street over, where the lighting was better and local boys could be hired to watch the Pontiac.

Jeff placed a finger next to the outline of a building two doors from the garage compound. "Mrs. Agrigento's place. Correct, Lieutenant?"

Although the Libyan lieutenant's expression didn't change, his eyes cut quickly toward Jeff and me, the glance of a fellow conspirator in sexual commerce. "You know the souk well, my Captain. I was informed so by my chief."

"Point is," Jeff said, "don't all these places have more than one door?"

"There's an alley out back," I added. "Look here, it's a thin line on the map. The madam's servant led us out that way one time when we'd been followed. Here and around to here. I'm betting the garage has a rear entrance, too."

"You betcha," Ops answered. "We go in from the front and the back."

"You're not going anywhere, Colonel," the ambassador said. "You're staying here with me. If Mr. Harris calls, you're to deal with him. Stall him. Keep him on the line."

After a brief consultation between the Marine major, the police lieutenant and Jeff, we took off, driving through mostly quiet streets, encountering little traffic. Since the end of the Six-Day War, patrols had been stepped up. Wise citizens kept out of sight rather than lazing around on street corners or in markets. Although Wheelus was still officially on alert, the local workers who'd been barred during and immediately after the war were now allowed back. Officers and noncoms don't like making their own beds, fueling airplanes or cleaning toilets. But the atmosphere of mutual distrust had hardened.

We halted briefly three blocks from the garage. Foot patrols and temporary barriers had cordoned off the neighborhood. After identifying ourselves, we parked, coordinated wristwatches and separated. Jeff, Sergeant Ward, the Marine major and one of his sharpshooters, a local police lieutenant and I were going in the back; a squad of riot police and half a dozen more Marines would tackle the doors in front. I'd started to sweat under the bullet-proof vest and helmet—nerves, adrenalin, gut-deep fear that Hal and Cotton had already been harmed—praying that we weren't too late. I was ready to fight. We had nine minutes.

Signora Agrigento's door didn't open for fully one of those minutes. At last, the peephole opened, she recognized Jeff and unbolted the door.

"I am not at home for visitors, gentlemen. I—" She stepped back when she saw the uniforms and weapons. "No, please."

"This ain't any social call, ma'am," Jeff said. "Where's your servant, the old woman?"

The young sharpshooter's mouth hung open. I guessed he'd never been inside such a classy bordello. The dives he visited probably lacked amenities such as polished brass tray-tables, hanging lanterns, silk carpets, huge floor pillows, potted palms and paintings of nearly naked belly dancers.

"Sabirah?"

"The garage down the street," I said. "There must be a rear entrance. She led us through the alley that night we were followed. Past there."

"Ah, of course." Mrs. Agrigento rang a brass bell on the table. "You're right. There must be. I wouldn't know. The alley, well—"

The old woman appeared. The madam spoke to her in a mixture of Italian and Arabic. Turning back to Jeff, she said, "Indeed, sir. There is such a door to the automobile garage. She will lead you to it."

"Tell her to hot foot it back here once we go through it," Jeff said. "Then lock all your own doors and wait for us by your own alley entryway."

"Yes."

"So we can get back in when we need to."

"If we do need to," the police lieutenant added.

Sabirah led us silently down the alley, pointed at a heavy metal door and retreated. The alley stunk of urine, garbage and mildew. The rotting corpse of a mangy dog lay on a trash heap behind the garage.

Jeff and the Marine major checked their watches. "Thirty seconds," Jeff said. "Twenty, fifteen, ten, eight, six, five, four, three, two, go, go, go, go."

The door was unlocked and opened inward. It was blocked by a body wedged against it.

Oh, Christ, not Hal, not Cotton, not my boy.

The body was Ma'amoud's. His throat had been cut. His shirt was hiked up under his arms, his pants bunched around one ankle. He'd been raped and killed, or maybe the other way round. As I tried to step over his body, I slipped in the sheet of blood surrounding his neck, head and chest.

Be a hee-ro and fall on your butt, Joe.

Regaining my balance, both hands now firmly gripping the pistol, I moved beside Jeff and the major and sighted down the long, left side of the two-lane bay. Sergeant Ward, the local lieutenant and the sharpshooter took the right side.

Hal and Cotton lay naked on a filthy mattress, bound together with leather belts, the boy spooned behind the man as if fucking him. Crouching beside them, halfway down the room, Fritsche aimed an automatic pistol in our direction. Fritsche, Harris, Jay, whatever his real name, the man's bare chest, arms and hands were smeared with blood.

Hal yelled, "Joe."

"Rocky."

Shots hit metal somewhere beyond the garage bay. The door to the front office was kicked in and royalist troops and Marines began swarming into the bay through a narrow door.

Behind Fritsche, a thug wearing the uniform of an airman second and a dark-faced, middle-aged local—the garage owner, we found out later—brandished a tire iron and a huge monkey wrench. Sergeant Ward dropped the bogus airman with one shot. The garage owner failed to survive what must have been a dozen shots fired by Marine guards and the police. Fritsche swung right and winged the Marine at Ward's side. The wounded leatherneck started shouting, "Medic! Medic!"

Fat chance. This ain't Vietnam.

Fritsche turned his pistol toward Hal and Cotton and his eyes toward me and Jeff. "What about that truce, boys? Safe passage out? Cut our losses? They're coming for me."

"Nobody's coming, Mr. Harris," Jeff answered. "Been diverted back to Torrejon. Cut your losses, yeah, do that. Drop your weapon. Hands in the air. You."

All hope gone, Fritsche shouted, "I'll see you in hell, you tight-butted jerk-offs."

Hal, stronger than the two leather belts binding him to Cotton, finally broke free. Jumping up to shield Cotton, he took Fritsche's bullet and went down, silently clawing at his chest.

Fritsche turned toward me and Jeff but hesitated half a second too long. Maybe he couldn't decide which one of us to take with him.

I hit him with two shots, Jeff with three, the local lieutenant with three more. We never knew whose bullet killed him. It didn't matter. On this round, we weren't keeping score.

Hal groaned. Dropping my pistol, I knelt beside him, supporting his head with my hand. It was as close as I could come to embracing him without hurting him more.

Rasping, he said, "He didn't, Colonel Elmo, he didn't, you know, tell me about Ted, not enough. Maybe he was scared. Maybe he, Ted, hurt him, too, like he did us. I think I'm dying, Joe. My chest hurts so bad."

The room stank—gun smoke, blood, sweat, rancid oil and freshly released urine. I choked, could barely answer. "We got him, Rocky. He's dead. McAddams is going down. You'll be OK. We've got medics on the way."

"Pray for me, Joe. Will you pray for me? I don't think it was sin what we did. I think, with love, Jesus would—" and then he suddenly coughed up blood, a lot of it, drenching my pants, and tried to put his arm around me, and failed, coughed again and stopped breathing. His head fell back, and I lowered him as gently as I could.

Oh fuck, don't leave me, Rocky. Damn, talk about love. Don't die, Rocky. Please don't die. Don't you know how much I love you? I never told you. Please don't die on me.

Rough-handed marines and police medics carrying oxygen masks and stethoscopes suddenly shoved me out of the way.

Fritsche lay on his back, a few feet from Hal's body. I was dazed, blood crazed, only half consciously aware I'd killed the man who'd murdered one of my best buddies, so I didn't resist the temptation to inspect the tattoo on his arm. Even beneath a light coat of Ma'amoud's blood there was no doubt about the identification. Major Ted Fritsche, Agent Harris and Jay the Oilman were the same man. Jeff's remark about Nazi lampshades floated across my mind. Even without a tanned hide souvenir, I'd remember this tattoo the rest of my life: the woman's name, "Dorris," encircled by a bleeding heart.

I looked around. Cotton and Jeff were gone.

Aw, fuck, what now?

Sergeant Ward and the police lieutenant were suddenly beside me.

"Out this way, sir."

"Where's the boy? And Captain Masters?"

"Watch your step in the blood, sir. Here, turn right. Good."

They hustled me back up the alley to the bordello. There I found Cotton, now dressed in an oversize man's shirt and pants that were a foot too short. We embraced the way teammates do after a winning game, aware of being watched. Then Cotton began to giggle.

"What?" I whispered.

"Last time we got attacked," he whispered back, "I was treated like a hero. This time I almost got, you know, like, well, you know. In the rear."

"But you didn't?"

"Your friend wouldn't have done that. He promised."

"No, you're right. He wouldn't. He was a good man."

"Was? Oh, shit. Oh, no. Oh, fuck, no, no."

"Ma'amoud, too."

"I know. Couldn't watch. He screamed and screamed when the Major, you know, forced him. So I guess that's why he cut him."

Thirty minutes more, boy, and Harris or one of the others might have forced you. Thank God we got there in time.

The Marine detachment commander tapped me on the shoulder. Cotton's presence on the scene need not be generally known, he explained. An embassy car with a police escort was on its way to pick him up. His mother, reached by walkie-talkie, had ordered the major to accompany him to Wheelus hospital for a thorough evaluation.

"I'm really fine, sir. All I need's a shower and something to eat."

"Mama's orders, son. We don't have any choice."

"Come with me, Joe. OK?"

"I'll catch up with you at the hospital. Or the embassy. I've got things to take care of first."

Cotton suddenly looked fearful and exhausted. "Later, Hawk? Just us guys? Promise?"

"You got it, Crane. Just us guys."

Because it was a weekend, I had extra money in my wallet, about sixty dollars total. I gave forty to Mrs. Agrigento, twenty to the old woman.

"The body of the American ambassador's servant lies in the garage," I said. "She'll want him back, to give him a proper burial. Can you send a message or see to it? The embassy will pay."

The madam bowed her head and slipped the pair of worn twenties into her bra. "You are *un galantuomo, signore.* Such a man. And I will, of course, see to it. Forgive me for what I said before. Such a man. Such a man you are."

"The phrase the Company uses," I told Ambassador Boardman in her office at the embassy, "is 'termination with extreme prejudice.' From what I've read, most of it either classified or unsourced, the Company uses it primarily on locals and little guys who either know bad things or try to play both sides. Tossing gooks out of helicopters over the South China Sea, for instance. Sharks clean up the evidence."

I was dead tired. Hal's death had hit me hard and I hadn't even started to mourn yet. Although I'd washed up and put on a pair of Cotton's clean trousers, my body still smelled like spilled blood and gun smoke. All I wanted was to check on Cotton at the hospital, head for the BOQ, slug down a tumbler of Spanish brandy and sleep until Monday. But Elizabeth Boardman intended to deal with Colonel Swanson, now, tonight, before supper.

"It hardly seems possible," she said. "West Point. The War College. 'Duty Honor Country.' He hoped to make general next year."

"The colonel started out as genuine, silver-edged Air Force," Ops said. "Unlike your Major Fritsche."

I tried a joke. "I've got a stack of additional duties. Safety officer, administrative training officer, flight-line escort. One of his must have been wrangling fake officers."

Mrs. Boardman glanced at Ops. "Do you suppose there are more?"

"Anywhere, ma'am? Sure. Under my command? Besides the dead driver? It's possible. I can ask the OSI or USAFE inspector general to sift through our personnel files for ringers. Especially since General McAddams used Major Denman, may the Lord God save him, as his errand boy."

Errand boy? My One-Punch? He was a hero, a man. I am not going to break down and bawl, not in front of her, not in front of Ops.

"Fritsche was the errand boy," I said. "Carrying out the colonel's illegal orders."

"Joe, dear, do you really think—?"

Dear?

"Yes'm, I do. We can't prove that Fritsche killed Pete Ferrette. What he said, that Ferrette died because he hadn't fastened his belts, could be right. But Lieutenant Connolly recognized Fritsche after the crash. He served under Colonel Swanson and was murdered. So the colonel had to have signed off on it."

Ops swabbed his shaved dome with his hands. "The colonel might well argue he was just following orders from Washington."

"The Nuremberg trials," Mrs. Boardman said, "concluded that following illegal orders from Berlin did not justify war crimes."

"Both of them were protecting Ferrette's and then Fritsche's operation in Laos, ma'am. Our war."

"About which I was informed in general terms, Colonel."

"And the homemade operation downtown."

"About which I was not, as you know."

I decided I'd better come clean about the documents. "The flight plan on file from the crashed plane is fake. Somebody substituted a Dover-Wheelus-Dover plan after the accident."

The ambassador tapped the desktop with a finger. "I was aware that Pete was on his way to Laos, Joe."

"Yes, ma'am. That's what the original flight plan stated. The one in our operations file is as phony as Fritsche's commission."

"Can you prove this, Joe?"

"Carbon flimsies of the original flight plan, cargo manifest and crew and passenger lists are locked in my safe."

Ops didn't look happy. "You stole my documents, Joe? I can't—you should have told me sooner."

"The crash looked wrong from the start, sir. Lieutenant Connolly saw it but was too scared to talk about it—or about Fritsche. I asked my clerk to borrow whatever he could, copy everything and let me sort through it. When he tried to return the flimsies the next day, different documents had been inserted in the files. When it happened again, Connolly got scared and went to his sister at the Pentagon. She inadvertently dropped the news on the wrong man, Elmo McAddams, and that got her baby brother thrown off the Uaddan minaret by the locals."

"Besides the fake flight plan, the real documents told you what?" Ops's expression had softened a bit.

"Crew names were different from what I heard at the crash site. Couple of documents were missing altogether."

"You just walked into my shop and lifted documents?"

"Sir, I have a clerk who is extremely good at handling classified materials and administrative details."

Mrs. Boardman tapped her finger on the desktop a second time. She got it, the source of my tip on Swanson's ribbon rack. But she said nothing.

"He also bribed your ops people to look the other way."

"Bribed? Joe, you—"

"With Dixie cups of banana ice cream."

Ops and the ambassador both laughed. "Colonel," she said, "you have several excellent young officers in your command. You may want to consider forwarding recommendations that Joe and Captain Masters be officially commended for to-day's events, perhaps awarded medals."

Ops looked at me and winked. "My first priority Monday morning, ma'am."

"And Major Denman. Posthumous. It may help his family in some way."

"Exactly my thought, ma'am."

"He has a mother," I said. And then I almost did start to bawl. "Rocky was all she had."

Elizabeth Boardman leaned forward. She was a mother, too, and she'd almost lost her only son that afternoon. "Colonel, with your permission, may I recommend that Joe escort Major Denman's body home?"

Tears began running down my face when Ops answered, "Nothing could be more fitting, ma'am. I wish I'd thought of it myself."

Elizabeth turned away and let me cry. Ops dug in his pocket and handed me a clean, folded handkerchief.

After a couple of minutes, I pulled myself together. "It's going to take me a while," I said. "Losing a buddy. Having him die while you're holding him."

"Then let's finish this up, gentlemen." The ambassador picked up the house phone on her desk. "Jackie, we're ready for Colonel Swanson. Kindly ask Captain Masters to escort him in. Oh? He posted guards on the doors? Of course. Very prudent. Excellent."

Colonel Swanson marched into the room as if he owned it. As was proper, Ops and I came to attention. Ops did not salute and I followed his lead. Jeff, still in his bloody uniform, shoulder holster and pistol, walking a pace behind Swanson, came to attention and saluted the ambassador. Swanson did neither.

The ambassador tapped the desktop once again. We all knew insubordination when we saw it. "Colonel, I believe Captain Masters has read you your rights. You have, for example, the right to remain silent."

"Yes, Liz, he read me. It makes no difference."

Liz, not Winston Boardman's Lizzy. Only lovers would have the nerve to use pet names on this woman.

"Joe, take a chair. You've had a very long day. Colonel, I must inform you that very serious charges will be filed against you."

"It makes no difference."

"It will be alleged that, with apparent indifference to the interests and policy of the United States, you aided and supported the formation of a group whose sole purpose is the overthrow of the legitimate government of this country, a sovereign state."

"We get rid of King Aimless and we get more oil. You know that."

"It will be alleged that you were complicit in the murder of one of your officers."

Leaning forward, Swanson put his hands on her desk. Jeff put his right hand on his pistol. "Liz, think about it. You go forward with this reckless foolishness and I'll take you with me."

"Take your hands off my furniture, sir."

"You knew all about the Laos operation. You knew all about mortars for the brigade. You knew Fritsche was a ringer from the get-go."

Elizabeth glanced at Ops. "Laos, yes. The major's role, yes, as I told you. The rest, no."

Swanson's hands had become fists. "Moral lapses and serious misjudgments, Liz."

"How dare you?"

"Allowing your underage son to consort with an adult officer in private and without supervision, scandalizing decent people."

Christ, why don't you just kill us both, Colonel?

Swanson's voice was that of a determined prosecutor, not a prisoner in the dock. "Obstructing the continued operation of a classified program that was ultimately for the benefit of the United States of America and approved by much higher authority than your exalted self."

Ops stared at the floor and swallowed hard. Elizabeth looked as if she'd been slapped.

She was right. I'd had a long day. I'd had enough. "Wearing unauthorized decorations, Colonel?"

He turned on me. If his eyes had been pistols, I'd have been dead. "Stay out of this, boy."

"The Vietnam Service Ribbon, to be precise. On your chest."

The display of unearned decorations is a supremely dishonorable act, a severe breach of military protocol, technically permissible only if specifically authorized in order to complete some operation or mission-in-disguise. All of us knew it.

"You string-bean bastard puppy. Real men don't pay attention to crap like that. My ribbon racks are made up from an official list supplied by the Department of the Air Force to the manufacturer."

Now Elizabeth had had enough. "I consulted Colonel Opstein about this matter, sir. And he advised me to contact my superiors at State. They in turn urgently requested that the Department of the Air Force and the manufacturer provide lists of your authorized decorations."

"It's bull crap, Liz. Who dug this up? Joe?"

"I received word only yesterday, in a coded message. Colonel Opstein will no doubt see his confirmation when he returns to headquarters."

"Liz, you—"

"I am talking to you, sir. Allow me to finish. You yourself, not the department, supplied the list to the ribbon-rack company. Your signed cover letter is in their files. *Air Force Times* is going with the story."

"*Air Force Times?*"

"Other media will pick it up. This can't be stopped."

"I'm leaving now." Swanson's voice was low and calm. He must have thought he was still in charge.

Ops moved between Swanson and the door. "Your flight has been cancelled, Colonel."

Swanson tried to elbow past him. "Stand aside, Ops." Suddenly he tried to shove Ops against the desk. Jeff and I grabbed him from behind.

"Fritsche or Harris or whatever his real name is," I yelled. "He's dead. Wheelus and Idris are shut down."

"By whose orders?"

"Mine," Ops answered, brushing off his fatigues with his hands. "Madam Ambassador—her action to be confirmed by USAFE and NATO—an hour ago named me acting commander of all United States forces in Libya. Incoming flights have been diverted."

Elizabeth opened the top drawer of her desk. Beside a note pad, two lipsticks and assorted pens and pencils lay a Colt .32-caliber general's pistol specially modified with white rubber grips. "You, sir, have five minutes to make up your mind— whether you are placed under arrest or choose to take a military man's way out. There is no other way for you."

Elizabeth was almost out the door when Swanson's parting words stopped her. "Nothing's secret in this town, Liz. Or in Washington. Or Langley. Your precious boy's *situation* has been duly noted."

Fucking bastard. My career in ashes, Cotton's not yet begun, Elizabeth's ruined by scandal.

"Fortunately, Colonel, the close friendships I approve for my son will no longer be of any concern to you. Do I make my point?" She glanced at her wristwatch. "You have five minutes."

Swanson didn't answer. Ops, Jeff and I followed Elizabeth out into the corridor.

Swanson took about three minutes to decide. Seating himself in Elizabeth's desk chair, he put the pistol's muzzle in his mouth and aimed for his brain. Bone fragments, white brain tissue and blood destroyed a fine set of Scalamandré silk draperies behind his head, a handmade Libyan rug and, of course, the upholstered chair.

When we heard the shot, Elizabeth turned her face away. After thirty seconds, her voice shaking and very low, she whispered, "I will want sworn statements from each of you, detailed statements that will satisfy the departments of State and Defense. Cover everything—in particular the events of today and Colonel Swanson's connections to Agent Harris and to the deaths of Lieutenant Connolly, Mr. Ferrette, the men who died at the Wheelus bakery and the British Royal Army's camp."

She covered her face with her hands, took a couple of deep breaths and turned to Jeff and me. "Thank you for saving my son. We are in your debt forever. Captain Masters, you may call the police now. Joe, I'd like you to accompany me to the hospital. Jackie will find someone to follow with your car."

CHAPTER 14

THE DEAR LOVE OF COMRADES

Ambassador Boardman's car was a standard nine-passenger Cadillac Fleet-
wood limousine: sable black, leather seats, plush-covered foot rests and a
glass privacy panel separating passengers from driver.

The privacy panel stayed shut throughout the ride.

"A terrible day," the ambassador whispered, looking away, saluting the Marine
guard as we exited the embassy grounds. "A dozen or more dead."

"Cotton is alive. Not a scratch on him, that I could see. He sounded fine."

"Your friend is dead. A tragedy." Elizabeth's customary bored, diplomatic tone
was entirely absent.

"And your servant." There seemed no reason to tell her that Ma'amoud had
betrayed her trust, possibly more than once. Or that he had been raped. "Major
Denman took Cotton's bullet."

"I must write to his mother. You shall hand-carry my note, if you will."

"A pleasure, ma'am."

"I never met him, did I?" She opened a compartment in the armrest, drew out
a silver hipflask, opened it, drank and handed the flask to me. "And I shall spend
the rest of my life thanking heaven that a stranger sacrificed his life to save my son.
It's too terrible."

The brandy, presumably French and ten times smoother than the Spanish rot-gut Hal Denman had used to seduce me, was like nothing I'd ever tasted: brown sugar and butterscotch to start, with hints of jasmine and orange rind going down, but then smoke, the sweaty scent of a man and, finally, hot blood.

"Oh, Hal." I almost gagged and the tears started again. "No, you didn't meet him," I whispered. "Not that I know of."

"You don't care for the Cognac?"

I shook my head. "It's not that. Just ... Hal. Cotton. Ma'amoud. Ron Connolly. The whole—" I was going to say "fucking fuck-up" but caught myself.

"Cotton never met him, either? Your friend?"

Even dead tired, I could see where that line of inquiry might go, and headed it off. "Major Denman and I worked closely together on base. Other than dinners at the Swan, and a couple of trips to Rome, he seldom left Wheelus. He ran the personnel office. That didn't involve much local or diplomatic contact."

I took another swig and handed back the flask. She drank, capped it and returned it to its hiding place.

"It's difficult," she said, "to accept how much I trusted these people. And how casually my trust was abused. By Ferrette, by Harris, by—" Waving her hand, she broke off, clearly unwilling to name Colonel Swanson.

"I should have told you everything. Told you soon as I knew it."

"Beyond the information you and Captain Masters provided about the Sharia group and the colonel's decorations?"

"About women."

She patted the armrest, perhaps considering a third drink. "Women?"

"I didn't feel it was my place, ma'am. Especially after what Cotton said last Easter."

"This isn't easy to listen to, Captain Harding."

Captain Harding? Uh-oh. Watch it.

"He was my superior, ma'am. As his exec, it was my job to ignore certain things that went on in the office."

"In his private office? On base?"

"I figured if I'd said anything, the women wouldn't have backed me up. It'd have been my word against his. They were military. Enlisted women."

"You might have warned me."

"You took the warning about the colonel's medals seriously enough. But you didn't put a leash on Fritsche, Harris, whatever his name was. Not even after Jeff and I warned you."

"My instructions from State were to give Agency operatives a fairly free hand."

"Excuse me, ma'am. It's likely Pete Ferrette was terminated and that Agent Harris had a hand in it. We warned you about that."

"I was waiting for confirmation as to a connection between Fritsche and the colonel. As I said, my trust was misplaced."

I needed to piss and we were only halfway to Wheelus. The Cognac had dulled my caution. The words just popped out. "The CIA pisses on the military like we're a bunch of fire hydrants. They probably don't think too highly of diplomats, either. Normal rules don't apply."

"A lesson learned, yes. What, sir, have you learned out of all this?"

"Pardon my French."

"Lessons, my dear Joe?"

"In this country, as far as the U.S. goes, you're the boss. I should have told you what I knew when I first knew it. I keep too many secrets. That's how I was raised."

"About the women?"

Hell, even my secrets have secrets. I hope to hell I can keep enough of them safely tied down to get through this assignment.

"I meant about Agent Harris," I said, "when I first knew he was playing two roles. About the Pentagon general and his links to Hal and Harris."

"About Cotton, my son, who is all I have?"

"Basically, it's all my fault—putting Cotton in danger, letting him get snatched and almost—Christ, I couldn't have lived with myself. Not if—"

"Would you have told me that you and Cotton had been—intimate? From what he didn't say, and the tale his father told, I assume you were."

"No, ma'am, I wouldn't have told you. Not on what I knew then. None of it seemed connected. It was private."

"But you were?"

"Intimate? Yes."

"Often?"

"Twice. We—"

She cut me off. "Cotton claims you're his hero, that you saved each other and therefore belong to each other. I believe it's all just a schoolboy crush. Do you believe him? I'm not doubting your bravery or negating my lifelong debt to you for saving his life, not once but twice. But the differences in age and maturity are enormous."

This is it. Say it. Go.

"I do believe it, ma'am. I do believe we belong to each other. I can't think of any other way it could be."

Pressing a button, she rolled down the power window on her right. Hot fresh air filled the car. After two or three minutes she raised the window. "And your military career, Joe? Aren't the two entirely incompatible?"

The odds were on her side. But I favored optimism. "Not necessarily," I said. "Anyhow, Cotton's got college. Or else he gets drafted."

"Graduation would be five years away."

"I've put in for Vietnam. Not every man gets out alive. But I need to serve a tour there now, or soon as I can. Tonight, I'm riding with you to see the boy we both care about the most in the world. Tomorrow I've got to pack for Detroit. Take it a day at a time."

"This changes everything, you know."

"Doesn't change what I feel."

"That you feel so strongly about it, him, I mean, about Cotton. But he's not staying here. It's too dangerous. As soon as it can be arranged, I'm sending him back to his father in Virginia. Just until the start of the school year at Le Rosey."

"We were looking forward to tennis on your court, ma'am. And we still haven't seen the Roman ruins at Sabratha."

I didn't want to argue or beg. After two close calls, what she said made sense.

"If I may make a suggestion, Joe."

"Ma'am?"

"Don't come running right back here after Major Denman's funeral. Put in for two weeks' leave. Visit your family in Florida for a few days. Cotton and I will meet you in Palm Beach. It's off season, so no one will be there. One of the nice hotels must stay open during the summer. I'll wire you the details."

The Cognac kept me steady. I almost couldn't breathe. "That sounds fine," I finally answered. "I'm looking forward to it already. I've never been to Palm Beach."

"And perhaps another visit next summer. Not in Libya. Some resort hideaway, perhaps Hawaii. We'll see."

Or maybe Michigan, I thought, *to visit Hal's grave.*

Two hours later, when I finally entered my BOQ room, I found a note slipped under the door.

*Joe, word's out you've had a rough day. Can't seem to get
my door to lock. If you want to drop by and help me fix it, that'll
be rockin. Sam*

Sam's Goldman's room was one building over. I took the bottle of Spanish brandy with me. We did manage to lock his door. Although Sam was young he was also wise. He poured the drinks, listened to everything I had to say, took me to bed and held me in his arms until I slept.

"Assholes like him don't ever get shot," Jeff said. "Comes down to it, Agent Bivens and his kind ain't worth shooting."

It was Tuesday afternoon. I was leaving for Detroit the next day. Hal Denman's body would travel in the TWA jet's cargo hold, Captain Harding in the main cabin. We'd be met in New York and the casket transferred to a plane bound for Michigan. After two weeks' leave in Florida, I'd be off to my newly posted assignment in Southeast Asia.

We were walking back to the BOQ after filing copies of our statements with the OSI. The accounts, though not identical, swore to the truth of the same stories: Major Hal Denman's bravery and heroic sacrifice, Agent Harris's murderous treachery and General Elmo McAddams's perfidy and betrayal of subordinates. We ended by commending the admirable teamwork displayed by Air Force, Marine Corps and Royal Police forces in saving a VIP from harm and helping break up a dangerous band of dissident locals. Four single-space pages each, the statements were intended to dovetail with Ambassador Boardman's statement on Colonel Swanson's crimes and deceptions and Major Rae Connolly's findings on McAddams and the murder of her brother.

Jeff wanted to talk. "All them words, Joe. But what's the chances either one of us, or Rae or, shit, even Bivens will ever know what really happened to Ron Connolly or who did it?"

"The spooks and their friends got him, but I guess we'll never know the details."

"What about the kid?"

"What about him? He's eighteen. I told you. If he dropped out of school tomorrow and went back home, he'd get drafted. Anyway, Mama, Cotton and I came to an agreement. He's got college coming up. I've got Vietnam. Depending on when I can get R&R, we'll all meet somewhere next summer and see how we feel."

"So you wait at least a year and then get together with his mom playing chaperone."

"We've talked it through. He's still a schoolboy. I can wait."

"You think he's worth it? This ain't going to be easy."

"I don't think it. I know it."

Back at the BOQ, I shaved, showered, splashed a modest amount of Eau Sauvage on my neck and, despite the summer heat, dressed in formal civvies: a coat and tie. I was headed to the embassy for a private supper for three.

On my way out, I stopped to inspect a framed black-and-white photo of a crew-cut youth in boxing gloves, trunks and boots. Hal Denman had just won his Golden Gloves title. The referee held his victory hand aloft. I'd managed to lift a few such souvenirs and a stack of letters from Hal's rooms before the Air Police arrived to seal the doors.

I'm not sure I believed in God at that point. But I did as my buddy had asked. I got down on my knees and prayed for Hal Denman's immortal soul. He'd taken Cotton's bullet. I'd invite Cotton to join me in this ritual once we were together for good. By then, he'd be able to understand all of it: that in my short, fast, hectic life, I'd been fortunate enough to love and be loved by more than just one very brave and heroic man.

AUTHOR'S AFTERWORD

Some years ago, the brother of a man I knew, a CIA employee, jumped or was pushed from the roof of a resort hotel. A covert arms deal in which he may or may not have been involved had recently been discovered and exposed. The surviving brother, whose connections reached the highest levels of the government of the United States, made repeated inquiries about his otherwise happy-go-lucky sibling's death. The Agency stood firm in its explanation: suicide, reasons unknown, details classified. The nosy brother's promising military career was swiftly and summarily destroyed.

Unlike Joe Harding's encounter with the Agency, the arms were not British mortars, nor was the hotel located in Libya. CIA involvement with Libyan anti-royalist forces in the late 1960s is unclear and no doubt also classified. I mention the matter because the adventures of Joe Harding and his men, recounted here, just might have happened in some similar form or fashion. To tell their story I have silently rearranged the command structure and real estate of Wheelus as well as certain neighborhoods and agencies of Tripoli and Libya. While several institutions existed as described—the Uaddan Hotel and Casino, the Swan restaurant, the O-Club bar—the characters and situations in this novel are entirely my own invention and not based on any particular individuals or incidents.

Katharine V. Forrest, to whom this novel is dedicated, has by example as well as blue pencil taught me the value of coherent plot, well-honed narrative and skin-tight dialog. Steve Berman, my friend as well as my editor at Lethe Press, granted me considerable latitude in preparing this and other works for publication. Joe

Johnson and Ensan Case, tough guys with world-class literary sensibilities, read the next-to-final draft and reacted with intellectual force and scholarly discernment. Their suggestions improved almost every page of the manuscript. Stan Zielinski, Jim Duggins and Nathalie Dupree also offered valuable advice. Finally, a shout-out to book designer Toby Johnson, as always a joy to work with.

ABOUT THE AUTHOR

Elliott Mackle served four years in the United States Air Force during the Vietnam era, achieving the rank of captain. He was stationed in California, Italy and Libya, the latter the setting for *Captain Harding and His Friends,* a sequel to the multiple-award-winning *Captain Harding's Six-Day War* (2011). *Hot off the Presses* (2010), a romantic exposé of the racial and sexual politics surrounding the 1996 Centennial Olympic Games, is based in part on his adventures as a staff writer for the *Atlanta Journal-Constitution*. The newspaper's dining critic for a decade, he also reported on military affairs, travel and the national restaurant scene. His first novel, *It Takes Two* (2003), was a finalist for a Lambda Literary Award. He has written for *Travel & Leisure, Food & Wine, Los Angeles Times, Florida Historical Quarterly, Atlanta* and *Charleston* magazines and was a longtime columnist at *Creative Loafing,* the South's leading alternative newsweekly. Mackle wrote and produced segments for Nathalie Dupree's popular television series, *New Southern Cooking,* and authored a drama about gay bashing for Georgia Public Television. Along the way, he managed a horse farm, served as a child nutrition advocate for the State of Georgia, volunteered at an AIDS shelter, was founding co-chair of Emory University's GLBT alumni association and taught critical and editorial writing at Georgia State University. He lives in Atlanta with his partner of 40 years.

Also available from Lethe Press

CAPTAIN HARDING'S SIX-DAY WAR

by Elliott Mackle

Assigned to baby-sit a loose-cannon colonel at remote Wheelus Air Base, Libya, handsome, hard-charging Captain Joe Harding spends his off-duty time bedding an enlisted medic and a muscular major, then begins a nurturing friendship with the American ambassador's teenage son. The boy swiftly develops a crush on the man, feelings that Joe, a Southern gent with a strong moral sense, feels he cannot acknowledge or return. Joe's further adventures and misadventures during the course of the novel involve a clerk's murder, a flight-surgeon's drug abuse, a fist-fight in the officers' club bar, a straight roommate whose taste for leather gets him in trouble, the combat death of Joe's former lover, and participation in an all-male orgy witnessed by two very married but somewhat confused fighter jocks.

In the run-up to the 1967 war, a mob attacks the embassy in nearby Tripoli and the deranged colonel sets out to attack an Arab warship. To bring the pilots and their airplanes safely home – and keep the United States out of the war – Joe has two choices: either come out to his closest, straightest buddies or know himself to be a coward, a failure and a traitor to everything that he holds dear.

CPSIA information can be obtained at www.ICGtesting.com
Printed in the USA
LVOW13s1634140114

369395LV00010B/1322/P